# Aroma Holiday

## A NORA BLACK MIDLIFE PSYCHIC MYSTERY
## BOOK 7

## RENEE GEORGE

BARKSIDE OF THE MOON PRESS

Aroma Holiday

A Nora Black Midlife Psychic Mystery Book 7

Copyright © 2022 by Renee George

Publisher: Barkside of the Moon Press

Print: Jan 2023

ISBN: 978-1-947177-46-8

# PARANORMAL MYSTERIES & ROMANCES

## BY RENEE GEORGE

### Nora Black Midlife Psychic Mysteries

Sense & Scent Ability (Book 1)

For Whom the Smell Tolls (Book 2)

War of the Noses (Book 3)

Aroma With A View (Book 4)

Spice and Prejudice (Book 5)

Age of Inno-Scents (Book 6)

Aroma Holiday (Book 7)

Vapes of Wrath (Book 8)

The Scented Cipher (Book 9)

### Grimoires of a Middle-aged Witch

Earth Spells Are Easy (Book 1)

Spell On Fire (Book 2)

When the Spells Blows (Book 3)

Spell Over Troubled Water (Book 4)

Ghost in the Spell (Book 5)

# PRAISE FOR RENEE GEORGE

"Sense and Scent Ability by Renee George is a delightfully funny, smart, full of excitement, up-all-night fantastic read! I couldn't put it down. The latest installment in the Paranormal Women's Fiction movement, knocks it out of the park. Do yourself a favor and grab a copy today!"

——ROBYN PETERMAN NYT
BESTSELLING AUTHOR

"I'm loving the Paranormal Women's Fiction genre! Renee George's humor shines when a woman of a certain age sniffs out the bad guy and saves her bestie. Funny, strong female friendships rule!"

—-- MICHELLE M. PILLOW, NYT & USAT
BESTSELLING AUTHOR

"I smell a winner with Renee George's new book, Sense & Scent Ability! The heroine proves that being over fifty doesn't have to stink, even if her psychic visions do."

— -- MANDY M. ROTH, NY TIMES
BESTSELLING AUTHOR

"Sense & Scent Ability is everything! Nora Black is sassy, smart, and her smell-o-vision is scent-sational. I can't wait for the next Nora book!

— —MICHELE FREEMAN, *AUTHOR OF HOMETOWN HOMICIDE, A SHERIFF BLUE HAYES MYSTERY*

*For my husband and son.*
*I love our holiday traditions!*

# ACKNOWLEDGMENTS

A huge thank you to my "you saved my butt once again" crew of BFFs Robbin and Robyn for helping with their constant encouragement to get me to the end. Thank you for being my people! I love you guys!

To my editor Kelli Collins. You are a great friend and my rock! I'm sorry I am such a crap client. LOL (The woman is a saint, people!)

To the PWF #13 - Thanks for bringing attention to heroines of a certain age. You ladies are magnificent.

My husband Steve and my son Taylor for taking up the slack around the house, and most of all, leaving me alone to write! I literally couldn't do this without you.

My BFF Dakota Cassidy for being my one true heart when it comes to all things binge-worthy. I love you, girl!

And finally, to the readers. You are making this midlife writer happier than you can even imagine! Thank you for loving Nora and going on this journey with her and her BFF brigade.

**My name is Nora Black, and I'm having a very merry messy midlife Christmas!**

50s are the new 40s, and I'm living my best life ever. I may have a few more aches and pains, graying roots, and a couple of extra pounds, but I also have two quirky best friends who always have my back. Business is booming, and my love life has never been better or hotter.

That is until my sweetie Ezra Holden invited me home for Christmas to meet his family.

The season is full of surprises in Ezra's hometown, like a missing cousin, a case of mistaken identity, and a slew of painful memories—none of them my own.

This Holden Family Holiday should be filled with scents of peppermint, gingerbread, and pine, but all I smell is danger. It turns out my psychic nose really is the gift that keeps on giving.

# CHAPTER
# ONE

*December 23rd—2 days before Christmas*

**W**orld Famous Pork Tenderloin, a billboard on the right side of the road bragged. There was an accompanying picture of a sandwich stuffed with a deep-fried tenderloin, lettuce, tomatoes, pickles, and onions. The edges overlapped the plate.

"I haven't had a good tenderloin in years." I put my hand on Ezra's thigh as he drove north on Route 13. "Claiming to be world-famous is a bold brag, though. We could stop for lunch and put it to the test."

We were a few miles from Ezra's hometown of Hillside and in no hurry to get there.

The corner of Ezra's mouth quirked up. "First, they aren't being humble. It's the best tenderloin around. Second, you wouldn't be trying to use lunch to put off meeting my family, would you?"

"Me?" I took my hand back and pressed it to my chest. "I'm excited to meet your mother."

He chuckled. "I know what you sound like when you're excited, and this isn't it."

"I'm trying." I couldn't believe he'd asked me to go home with him for the holiday. Even more unbelievable, I'd said yes. "But my excitement or lack thereof has nothing to do with my stomach. I know we have dinner plans later, but I'm hungry now."

"I could eat," he said. "And we have time."

It was a little before noon. Later, we planned to attend the annual Christmas event in Hillside that started at four. After, we had dinner plans at the Oriental Palace Buffet with Ezra's parents and a handful of family, including his younger sister, Elaine. Elaine had recently separated from her husband, and she and her two young daughters had moved home with his parents.

Ezra and his sister were close, but that hadn't always been the case. Elaine was younger than him by five years. When Ezra had gotten his high school sweetheart, Kati, pregnant with their son Mason when he was sixteen, Elaine had been in elementary school.

Against his mother's wishes, Ezra, with his dad's reluctant consent, married Kati and moved in with her parents, Frank and Marla Martin. When he and Kati divorced a few years later, Ezra had supported himself doing factory work until he'd joined the police academy at the age of twenty-one.

He rarely traveled home to Hillside to see his family

and never around the holidays. As a matter of fact, this was his first Christmas back since he'd quit his job at the Springfield Police Department nine years earlier. He'd always used Mason as an excuse to stay in Garden Cove. I kind of felt like Mason was the reason he'd agreed to a Holden family Christmas this year. Ezra had been having mixed feelings about Mason going off to college a couple hundred miles away from Garden Cove. I think it made him more sympathetic to his own parents and how they must've felt when he moved away.

I saw another billboard touting the Hillside Santa Walk for Charity event. "I still can't believe that's a thing. Explain it to me again."

"Every year on December twenty-third, the town sponsors a parade of Santas to raise money for charity and collect food for families in need." A nostalgic smile played on his lips. "Traditionally, the mayor acts as the Grand Marshall, dresses like Santa and throws candy to all the kids from a float."

"And all the other Santas?"

He smirked. "People pay to dress up like Santa and walk in the parade. All that money goes to a charity."

"How much does it cost to do it?"

"Whatever they want to contribute, food or money. There's no minimum." He shrugged. "Hillside gets a couple hundred people in from all the surrounding areas who want to participate."

"So, a couple hundred dollars?"

"Try thousands. Mom told me they raised twenty-six thousand dollars last year."

I let out a low whistle. "That's a lot of Santas with deep pockets."

"The crowd donates as well, and Pike Manufacturing matches fifty percent of all donations."

Pike Manufacturing was the factory Ezra had worked in before going to the police academy. They made stainless steel appliances for commercial kitchens. It was the largest employer in Hillside.

Even so, it was still a lot of money to raise for one afternoon of dress-up. "And all the participants really sport Santa suits?"

"You get some elves, some Mrs. Clauses, and there was one guy who dressed like Krampus every year. Is it sad that I hope he's still around?"

I laughed. "Nope. Not sad. The event sounds like fun." The outside temperature on the car display read thirty-one degrees. "I wish it was warmer, though." The idea of standing outside for a long period of time in nearly freezing temperatures felt a little like torture.

"My dad and my Uncle Orsen have done the Santa walk since before I was born. We always go to the parade. My parents will expect us to go."

"I'm glad I brought warm clothes." I rubbed my arms, thinking about the cold but also what it was going to be like to meet his parents for the first time. "I don't want to disappoint your mom and dad."

"You won't." His gaze grew distant as if he were lost in thought.

"Are you nervous?" I asked him.

He raised a brow. "About them meeting you?"

"Sure." I realized I'd been holding tension in my shoulders for the entire ride. I rolled them back to get some relief, and there was a satisfying pop. "I mean, even if I wasn't...you know, me, it would still be a big deal, you know, taking someone home to meet the parents and all that jazz." Lord, I was rambling. Our age difference rarely came up, and between us, it hadn't been a problem. But now, he was taking me home to meet his mom and dad, who were both only a few years older than me. It made my age feel like a whole lot bigger issue.

Ezra pulled off MO-13 and into Weston's restaurant parking lot. "I'm not nervous about them meeting you." He put the car in park. "I've done so many things that have upset and frustrated them over the years. Bringing home a beautiful, successful, educated woman is going to be a huge improvement in their eyes."

"I think you're being really optimistic."

"If anyone says or does anything that makes you uncomfortable, we'll leave."

I nodded. "Okay." I hated the butterflies dancing around in my gut. I was too old to feel this insecure. My parents were both deceased, so I didn't have to worry about what they thought of me dating a man almost nineteen years my junior. Ezra, on the other hand, his parents, barring illness, were probably going to be around for a long time to come. If we stayed together, this was going to be an issue that I'd have to face over and over again. "It'll be fine," I assured him. "I'm certain we'll all get along."

Ezra snickered. "You overestimate my family's ability to get along, but I can promise you this, there is nothing that anyone could say or do that would make me give up what I have with you." He leaned across the seat to me, and I swear the air sizzled when his lips brushed mine. "I love you, Nora Black. You make me happy. That's the only thing I care about. Got it?"

I kissed him back, my stomach dipping as the pleasure of him washed over my body. "Got it," I said a bit breathlessly.

"Good." He patted my knee, then sat up and got out of the car.

We'd been on the road for almost four hours, so I was glad to get out and stretch. As I gathered my purse from the floorboard, he walked around to my side and opened the door for me. A whoosh of cool air rushed inside the car.

I swung my legs out and stood. "Dang, it's freezing out here."

The restaurant was a large building with brown siding and a beige metal roof with a low pitch. The parking lot had at least a dozen other cars and trucks in the lot.

"It's busy." I zipped my burgundy puffer coat all the way up and pulled up the collar.

"There'll be room." Ezra put his arm around my shoulders. "It's got a lot of seating inside." He gave me a squeeze. "Come on."

The large windows were flocked at the edges. Cling-film candy canes and snowmen were stuck in the centers of the panes, and there was a cling-film wreath on the glass front door that made me snicker. Gilly and Pippa had gone all out on decorations at Scents and Scentsability, our shop in Garden Cove. When I got home from this trip, it was going to take a week to take all the decorations down. Cling stickers would have been so much easier.

When we first walked into Weston's Restaurant, I braced myself for the inundation of aromas.

*"I'm getting the last onion ring." A man reaches out to a nearly empty plate, and a woman slaps his hand away with a hearty laugh.*

*A child runs around a table playing tag with another child as cherry pie is served to two adults.*

*"It's over." A woman stands up from the table, knocking over a cup of black coffee. "I'm leaving you."*

*"If I can fit this entire piece of chocolate cake into my mouth," another woman says, "then you have to take me out dancing Saturday night at the Tire Iron."*

*The guy across from her says, "If you can fit that whole thing in your mouth, then I'll marry you on Saturday."*

There were a half dozen more small memories, significant to their holders but relatively meaningless to me. As usual, I couldn't see any of their faces. They were blurred out like how Hollywood does with people who don't sign a release form on reality shows. After two years plus of seeing other people's scent-related memories, I'd gotten used to it. I took a few deep breaths and thought of my own memories. It helped clear away the cobwebs.

"You okay?" Ezra asked.

I smiled up at him. "Yep."

A thin older woman, probably in her mid to late sixties, with bright orange hair, stood behind a refrigerated dessert counter with over a dozen varieties of pies on display. The glorious sight of piled-high meringue, pecan pie, pumpkin pie, blackberry cobbler, apple pie and more was mouthwatering.

She gathered up two menus and two sets of napkin-rolled silverware and stepped out from behind. "Just the two of you?"

"Just the two of us," Ezra affirmed.

She gave us a genial smile and then nodded. "Follow me."

The hostess led us to a booth in the front corner. It was cold near the window, but I appreciated being able to see my car. Was I worried about vehicular theft? No, not really. But I'd packed away some presents for Ezra and his family in the back, including extra soaps and lotions from the shop, just in case there were people I hadn't accounted for, so it made me a little warier.

The hostess asked cheerfully, "Can I get you folks started with drinks while you look over the menu?"

"Diet coke with lemon," I answered.

"I'll have the same." Ezra took off his jacket and sat down. "Minus the lemon." He wore the teal green and black flannel shirt I liked so much. The blue-green color made his eyes even more vibrant.

After she left, I read through the menu. "Oh, man. They have fried okra."

"You should get some." He scanned his menu. "I'm having the tenderloin with fries and ordering onion rings to share."

"That sounds good, too." Truth was, just about everything on the menu sounded delicious, if not high-calorie and a little artery-hardening. I'd put on a few pounds over the past couple of months, but I'd decided to worry about that after the holidays were over. "I'll have the same."

A different server came back to our table with our drinks. "Here you go." She set the Diet Cokes on the table. "Are you all ready to order?"

I looked up from the menu. The server was another thin woman, but this one was in her thirties. She dug a pad and pencil out of her pocket. Her dark blonde hair was pulled back into a tight ponytail, making her angular features look sharp and hard.

"We'll have two tenderloin sandwiches with fries and an order of onion rings and fried okra." Ezra gave me a crooked smile. "You only live once."

I smirked and shook my head as I glanced back up at the server. "What he said."

She was staring at Ezra. "Easy?" Her brown eyes were alight with recognition. "Oh my gosh. Easy Holden?"

Ezra turned to look at her. He didn't register any recognition until she gave more detail about herself. "Trudy Donaldson, well, Harker now. From high school."

The creases around his eyes softened. "Trudy, yeah, hey. How are you?"

"Doing good," she said quickly. "Keeping busy."

"I see that." He gave a quick scan of the filled tables in the room. "Is this place still as good as I remember?"

"Still got the best sandwiches in the state," she crowed.

"In the world," I joked.

Ezra laughed. "Trudy, this is my partner, Nora Black."

We'd decided a while back that girlfriend and boyfriend were terms that didn't suit us, and we'd landed on the word partner.

However, Trudy mistook the meaning. "Oh, that's so nice. Are you a detective, too?" she asked me.

"No." I laughed softly. "Though, I have been known to dabble."

She gave us a confused look, and when I didn't explain more, she tapped her pad with the pencil. "I'll get your order in."

"Thanks." Ezra gave me a sly look. "Dabble, huh?"

"Do you think everyone is going to think I'm your work partner?"

"We can always come up with a better term if you want?" He leaned forward and put his elbows on the table as he stared at me with those hypnotizing green eyes. "My better half, my lover, my more-than-friend, my old la—"

I snapped my gaze to his. "Not if you like living."

He chuckled. "The yin to my yang, my reason for getting out of bed." He wiggled his brows. "My reason for getting into bed."

I nearly choked on my soda. "You're ridiculous."

"Ridiculously in love with you," he agreed.

I rolled my eyes, but I'll admit, I was "ridiculously" pleased. Ezra knew how to assure me in a way that didn't leave any room for interpretation. "Partner is fine." I put my hands in the middle of the table, and Ezra took them. "People can think what they want."

The restaurant had some Christmas decorations inside, including a giant Santa, but the walls were mostly adorned with old tin signs, taxidermized deer heads and wild turkeys, along with autographed pictures of silver screen stars and country music singers. Thick wooden beams crossed the vaulted ceilings, and there were fans recessed into the spaces. None were turned on, thank heavens. It was cold enough without a breeze. There were sports on several different televisions, but the volume was down as music played softly in the background.

I watched as Trudy brought a tray of food out and distributed it to a family of five sitting a few tables away from us. One of the plates had a tenderloin sandwich on it, and I was happy to see there was still some truth in advertising. Damn, it looked tasty.

"Yum." I pointed toward the table.

Ezra looked where I indicated, and the smile on his face faded. His brows knit close, creasing the skin between his eyes as his focus intensified.

"What's wrong?" I pressed his fingers to get his attention. "Do you know that family?"

"What?" He turned his gaze to me and then shook his head before looking back in that direction. "Not them. But I know the people sitting on the other side of them at that small table."

I scanned past the family to a couple. The man had a tall torso and was broadly built. He had thick dark hair and a short, well-groomed beard. The woman was youngish, probably in her late twenties or early thirties, and she had wavy blonde hair, striking dark eyebrows, and a narrow face.

"Who are they?" I asked him.

"The man is my sister's soon-to-be ex-husband."

"Oh." I nodded for him to go ahead. "And the woman? I take it she's not your sister."

"Nope." Ezra frowned. "That's my cousin Penny Carlson."

"You're Aunt Lettie's daughter?" He had given me the family rundown after I'd said yes to the trip. Aunt Lettie, his mom's sister, had three children. Penny was the oldest of the bunch.

Ezra nodded, his face reddening as the soon-to-be-ex Rob leaned over and laid his fingers across cousin Penny's forearm.

Ezra let go of my hand and stood up from the booth.

Oh, boy.

# TWO

"Ezra," I cautioned. However, I didn't move to stop him. My guy was not hasty or impulsive. He didn't act out of anger. He wasn't a rash man.

Which is why I was completely taken by surprise when he strolled across the restaurant and grabbed his startled soon-to-be-ex-brother-in-law's shoulder, and demanded, "Just what the hell are you playing at, Rob?"

Rob gaped at Ezra, astonishment plain on his face. "Easy?"

"Oh my, God. Easy?" Cousin Penny scooted back in her chair and stood up. "I am not doing this," she said. "Rob, I'm sorry. I just can't."

"You need to tell me why you're here with him," Ezra demanded.

"That's none of your business," she announced.

Ezra gestured to Rob. "Since this fool is still married to my sister, it is my business."

Their voices were raised loud enough to get the attention of the other diners. I debated on intervening, but Ezra trusted me to handle my stuff. I'd trust him to handle his.

"Now, take it easy, Ezra." Rob held out his hands in a "calm down" manner. Apparently, he was smart enough to keep his own emotions in check. "I know this looks bad, but there ain't—"

"No." Penny cut him off. "You don't owe him an explanation." She looked back and forth between the two men. "Besides, this is over."

"Now, Penny, don't—"

"No," she said firmly. "Over and done. I don't know what I was thinking."

"We can have this conversation now, or...." Ezra narrowed his gaze at her as he removed his hand from Rob. "Would you rather do it in front of all of our family at dinner tonight?"

Penny's eyes widened, and she looked genuinely afraid as she grabbed her purse and fled to the bathroom. Since it didn't look like the men would come to blows, I grabbed my purse and went to check on her.

There was a chicken on the women's restroom door with a sign above it that spelled, Hens. I imagined the men's bathroom had a rooster. Inside, there were five stalls, four regular and one handicap. I could hear sniffling going on behind the second closed stall door. One thing I wasn't going to do was try to talk to someone while they were on the toilet.

Instead, I went to the sink and washed my hands. I looked at myself in the mirror, horrified by the way the LED lighting washed out my skin. After drying my hands, I took a tinted lip balm, no scent, from my purse and dabbed a little color on my cheeks before applying it to my lips, then reassessed. Still bad, but better.

There was a nose blow and a toilet flush before Penny came out to the sinks. She barely looked at me, her eyes red and puffy, as she washed her hands.

"Are you okay?" I asked.

"I'm fine." She gave me a suspicious glance before grabbing a few paper towels. "Or I will be." Penny took a bottle of cologne from her purse and pumped a fine mist in front of her, then leaned into it.

It had sweet notes of berries and bergamot, and the scent made my head spin.

*"You smell good enough to eat," a man says as he pulls a woman close. They're standing by a gold-flecked kitchen counter, a white fridge with a dent and a thick scratch on the top freezer door behind them. "Do you like it?"*

*The woman holds a bottle of cologne in her hand. She sniffs it. "I love it."*

*He nuzzles her neck. "God, how did I get so lucky?"*

*She wraps her arms around his waist. "I am a catch," she jokes.*

*"You are," he says. "And when this is all over, I'll make sure you have the life you always dreamed of."*

*"And we'll get Kyle?"*

*He kisses her. "Of course. We'll be a family."*

*"You make me so happy, Jay."*

*"And I plan to keep making you happy for as long as we live."*

*The undercurrent of near obsession choked me.*

"Are you all right?" Penny asked. "Your whole face went pale."

"It's the lighting." I gave my cheeks a light pinch. I knew I'd be running into her again, so I confessed my identity. "I'm with Ezra, by the way."

She sighed with mild frustration. "Of course you are."

"We drove up from Garden Cove for the family Christmas."

Penny's face relaxed a little. "Easy's always been bossy. I guess growing up as fast as he did does a number on you. But he hasn't been around for a long time, so he doesn't get to nose around in my business." She threw her paper towels in the trash. "I get that Aunt Lynn wanted him to come home this year, his dad being sick and all, but that don't give him a right to poke around in my business."

Was his dad sick? Ezra hadn't said. Maybe it was something he wasn't ready to talk about. I could understand that. When my mom first got sick, I had a tough time sharing the news with people. But, whether or not her being at the restaurant with Ezra's sister's ex not being his business was debatable. "Isn't Rob his brother-in-law?"

Her soft expression turned hard, and she fixed me

with a glare. "I wouldn't betray my family. Not like some people." It was a not-so-subtle dig at Ezra. "But, even if I would, it definitely don't give you any right to my business either." She held her purse to her body. "Look, you seem like a nice lady and all, but take my advice, don't put your nose where it don't belong."

She stormed out of the restroom the same way she'd come in, with a flourish.

I gave a quick salute to the backside of the door. "See you."

When I got back out into the restaurant, Ezra was sitting back in our booth, and both Rob and Penny were gone. I'm not sure what had transpired between them, but there were no tables overturned or chairs broken, and all the diners were back to enjoying their meals and each other. All good news.

Even better news, Trudy beat me back to the booth with the onion rings and the fried okra. I slid into my seat. "Wow, these look as good as they smell."

The corner of Ezra's lips tugged up into a sheepish smile. "They'll taste just as good."

I took one of the appetizer plates that Trudy had brought with the food and squeezed some catsup onto it. I took a thin-cut onion ring, its outer shell light and crispy, and did a quick dip before taking a bite.

Holy hells, I was not disappointed. "You need to learn how to make this batter." I didn't cook, but some-times he did.

Ezra picked up one of the onion rings. "I'll put it on my to-do list."

"This would be good as a fried chicken coating too. So crispy, almost like a shortcrust, but thinner and tastier. Perfect amount of seasoning as well. Salty with a slight peppery kick." I took another bite. "And the onion is thin and cooked to perfection."

My veracity for the onion rings seemed to lighten Ezra's mood. "We should see about getting Jordy to add it to the menu at the coffee shop."

Jordy Hines, the owner of Moo-La-Lattes in Garden Cove, was married to my business partner and bestie, Pippa. "I'm not sure we can convince him that scones and onion rings go hand in hand, but I would be there every day for it."

"You're already there every day."

"Uh-huh." I picked up a piece of fried okra and popped it into my mouth. Holy crap, it was excellent too. This was quickly becoming my new favorite restaurant. Minus the drama, of course. "So." I finished the bite. "You wanna talk about what happened over there?"

"The guy's married to my sister and out with my cousin. Pretty cut and dried." He arched a brow. "Unless you have some information that I'm not aware of."

"While we were in the restroom, Penny sprayed some cologne, I don't know how old the memory was, but she was in a romantic clinch with a guy named Jay." I gestured to the table where she'd been sitting with his brother-in-law. "Is that a nickname for Rob?"

"Not that I've ever heard."

"And she said something about someone named Kyle," I continued. "I'm not sure how he fits in the picture, but it sounded like it could be her kid, maybe."

"Her son Kyle," he confirmed. "The kid has to be ten or eleven now. His father got full custody when they split."

"Ouch."

"She was a mess back then," Ezra smirked. "Seems like she still is."

Trudy picked that time to bring our tenderloins. They were pounded thin, breaded to perfection, and way too big for the toasted bun. There was a side of steak cut fries, along with lettuce, tomato, pickles, and onions. "Here you go." Trudy set down a small tub of mayo. "Enjoy, you two."

"Thank you," I said with enthusiasm. "This looks awesome."

Trudy beamed. "Let me know if you need anything else."

"You got it." I spread mayo onto the bun, topped my tenderloin with all the fixings, then cut my sandwich in half. I rubbed my hands together because this was a hand-rubbing moment. "I've never been so excited about a sandwich before."

Ezra chuckled. "I see that." He finished putting his own together. "Were you able to talk to Penny?"

I shrugged. "She said she wouldn't betray family, then told me to mind my own business. That doesn't really scream, hey, I'm not having an affair, but there was also something in her tone. She sounded like someone...in trouble." I took a bite and melted into my seat. "Mmmmmm."

Ezra bit into his sandwich too. "Oh, yeah," he agreed mid-chew. "Just as good as I remember."

His eyes were pinched with worry as we finished our meal without any more conversation. Frankly, I was concerned too. I'd already been worried about meeting his family, but now that I knew his dad was sick, it was going to make things potentially more awkward. Regardless, Ezra was always there for me when I needed a rock or shelter, and he gave me space when I didn't. I could and would do the same for him.

We had planned to go directly to the local bed and breakfast first to check in before driving over to Ezra's childhood home to see his folks, but I wondered if some of his anxiousness was worry for his dad. He hadn't seen him for a while, and illness could take a toll.

I'd managed to plow through half my sandwich and a few of the fries, but my stomach was threatening to burst if I ate any more. I pushed the plate away from me so I wouldn't be tempted.

"I know we're supposed to meet your parents at two-thirty before going to the Santa Walk, but do you want to go by their house to check in before we go to the Thorny Creek Inn?" With Elaine and the girls staying at Ezra's parents, there hadn't been any room for us to stay there.

"No." He shook his head. "I'd rather go to the B and B first." He gave me a slight smile. "I'm kind of excited to stay there. I've always wanted to see the inside of it."

"It's been around for a while, huh?"

"For longer than I can remember. I've been out there a couple of times. Both times for outdoor weddings."

Since it was his hometown, I'd let Ezra make all the arrangements. I hadn't even bothered to look up the Thorny Creek Inn, but now I was curious. "It must be a pretty good-sized property if it's used for wedding venues."

"It's on twenty acres and only a mile out of town. Close enough to be convenient, but with the appeal of being out in the woods."

Ezra's cabin, where he lived now, was out in the woods. It was cozy and secluded, and he had his own small dock right on the lake. He loved being away from the bustle. I'd always thought the reason was because of his work. Dealing with people at their worst day in and day out could take its toll. My dad and my ex-husband had both been police officers, and the job had sometimes done a number on them. But he talked about the bed and breakfast as if the idyllic location had been something he'd always aspired to.

I gave a soft laugh. "You really don't like having neighbors, do you?"

He arched a brow at me. "Why? You trying to get me to move to town?"

I tried to keep the panic out of my eyes. "Not at all." I

liked our arrangement. We saw each other almost every day, and we spent most nights together going back and forth between my house and his cabin. Even so, I liked having a place that was just mine. I loved my independence almost as much as I loved Ezra, but for him, I might consider.... Why was he smirking at me?

"I can see the wheels about to come off in your brain, Nora. You don't have to worry. I'm not trying to move in with you or get you to move in with me. I like what we have just the way it is, same as you."

I resisted the urge to let out an audible *whew*. "I wasn't worried."

He snorted on a laugh, his grin widening. "Don't take up gambling because your poker face is awful."

"Ha ha," I said blandly.

Trudy came over with a pitcher of Diet Coke. "Can I top you off?"

"Just the check," Ezra replied. "I think we're done."

"Do you want a to-go box?" she asked me. Ezra had wiped out his plate.

"We wouldn't have anywhere to store it," I lamented. "But thank you. Everything was delicious."

As she walked away, we heard shouting and a car alarm. Ezra and I both turned to the window. Outside, very near my car, Penny was in a heated conversation with a stocky-looking man, though it was hard to tell his shape with all his winter gear on. He had tan canvas coveralls and a hood from a hoodie covering his head, His back was to us, so I couldn't see his face. He wasn't dressed the way Rob, the soon-to-be-ex, had been dressed in the diner, but that didn't mean anything. Rob could've put the coveralls on after he left.

The guy gave Penny a shove, and she stumbled back and fell to her butt. The man didn't make a move toward her. He was saying something, but his voice had quieted, and we couldn't hear him.

Penny, who looked stunned but not injured, called him a few choice words as she moved into a crouched position.

Ezra slid out of the booth. "Can you grab the check?"

"Go." I waved him out. "I've got this. I'll meet you outside."

I glanced back at the window, and Penny was gathering a handful of gravel in her hand.

"Don't do it," I heard Ezra say loud but firmly.

The man in the coveralls took off running.

"Hey!" Ezra shouted. "Stop."

The assailant hauled butt across the road to the gas station on the other side and disappeared around the back.

Penny got to her feet and dropped the rocks before putting out a hand to stop Ezra. Her face was angry as she spoke to him. I could imagine it was a whole lot more of "mind your own business" BS. Well, at least she wasn't hurt.

Trudy came back to the table with the check. She gestured toward Ezra and Penny. "That girl is chaos on a stick."

"You know Penny?" I asked.

"She was a few years younger than Ezra and me, but yeah. She's always been a little wild."

"Drugs?" I don't know why the thought popped into my head. Penny was skinny but not emaciated. Still, when it came to trouble, drugs were often involved.

Trudy shrugged. "Who knows?"

"What about Rob..." I couldn't remember if Ezra had told me his last name, so I added, "The guy she came in with."

Trudy's eyes widened with surprise. "Rob Phillips?"

"I guess that's him. Is he trouble?"

"In a different way," Trudy said. "He's HPD." When I raised my eyebrows, she explained, "Hillside Police Department. Rob's a cop."

CHAPTER
# THREE

E zra gripped the wheel, the leather squeaking under his hands as he drove into Hillside. The streetlights in town had been adorned with garland and wreaths, and outdoor holiday displays decorated the front of homes, businesses, and churches. We passed several barricaded streets with signs that mapped the closed-off route for the Santa Walk.

"Well, that was an interesting lunch," I said neutrally.

"Yep," he agreed. "Interesting."

Penny had taken off by the time I'd finished paying and had made it out to the parking lot. Since getting on the road, Ezra had been pretty quiet, and while I was usually great with a little silence, my concern for him was getting the better of me. "Are you okay?"

His lips were thin, and he watched the road through narrowed slits. "Mm-hmm," was his only reply.

"So, Trudy says Rob is a Hillside police officer. Did you know that?" I assumed he did, but I wasn't sure how much he checked in with his family. Maybe his soon-to-be ex-BIL had recently changed careers.

"Yep." Ezra nodded. "Knew it."

I wasn't put off by his short responses. At least he hadn't let his anger completely shut him down. "Was that Rob arguing with her in the parking lot?"

"It wasn't Rob," he said. "The guy was too short. She wouldn't say who it was, though."

My breath on the window fogged it up. I drew a smiley face in the condensation. "Your cousin seems pretty contrary."

My word choice made him smirk. "That's one way to put it." He took one hand off the wheel and rubbed his face. "Sorry. This holiday is starting off on the wrong note."

"Any holiday I spend with you is a good one." He turned onto a street going north. "I thought the Inn was on the west side."

"I think we need to stop by my parents' place first." He dropped his hand over mine. "You don't mind, do you?"

"Nope." After all, I'd already suggested it. "What changed your mind?"

"I just found out my dad's sick." His expression darkened. "Penny pointed out that I would know if I ever bothered to come home."

"I'm sorry." I rotated my body, turning my knees

toward the console to face him. I hated that I had learned the news about his father before him. I hated even more that his cousin had used the information as a weapon. "I thought his illness might be the reason you wanted to be here for Christmas."

He pulled up to a stop sign and gave me an odd look. "Did you know about Dad being sick?" His question was curious, not angry. "Was it your—" He touched his nose.

I shook my head. "Your cousin brought it up in the restaurant bathroom."

"Huh." He chewed on his cheek as he considered what to say next. He looked like he was teetering back and forth on how to feel.

I turned my hand so that our palms were together and laced my fingers with his. "I thought you weren't ready to talk about it. I remember how hard it was when my mom got sick. I figured you'd tell me in your own time."

Ezra's fingers curled against mine. "I appreciate the consideration, but for future reference, there's nothing that I wouldn't want to share with you. Good or bad. So, if you find out anything else while we're here, and I haven't told you about it, just assume I don't know and go from there."

"Noted."

He turned left, then two blocks down, he turned right. We ended up on a street bordered by small one and two-story bungalow homes. Several houses had Christmas lawn ornaments ranging from blow-up

Peanuts characters, the Grinch, Snowmen, Santa and his reindeer, elves, dragons, and nativities. It was quite the mix.

When Ezra began to slow down, he pointed at one of the larger homes on the block. It was a white two-story craftsman-style bungalow with a covered porch and a double driveway with a carport and a one-car garage on a corner lot. In the yard, Santa waved from his sleigh with his reindeer scattered about as if they were grazing.

With only a hint of trepidation, he said, "There's home."

"Cool. I love all the decorations. Your parents go all out."

"You should see it after dark. This house lights up like a colorful, blinky supernova." He parked on the curb outside the house. "We can drive by tonight after dinner so you can see it."

"That sounds good to me." I didn't make a move to exit the car. I wasn't sure how Ezra wanted this to play out. Did he want to talk to his mom and dad alone, or did he want me by his side? I wasn't sure how that was going to make his parents feel, but then again, their feelings weren't my priority. "I could wait out here if you want."

He took a deep breath and then shook his head. "I want you to come in with me. I'm not going to ambush them, but from what Penny said, Dad looks sick, so it's going to come up. We'll just go in for introductions and let the chips fall where they may.

I undid my seatbelt, leaned over, reached up and smoothed my thumb across his cheek. He pivoted his gaze to mine, and I could see the pain in them.

Right now, we only had his cousin's haphazard version of the story. Once we went in, we'd have more information to act on. I hoped it wasn't something chronic and fatal, but after taking care of my mother through the end stages of her cancer, I feared the worst. "You've got this," I told him. "And whatever you don't have, I've got."

The corners of his mouth turned up into a smile. "I know." He kissed me gently but quick. "I think someone's watching us from the window."

"Then we better go knock on the door."

"Yep."

"Are you stalling?"

"Maybe." He half-heartedly laughed. "We should've just gone to the inn. I don't know what I was thinking."

"You were thinking that your cousin just dropped a bombshell on you, and you needed to investigate. It's what makes you a good detective."

"But not a good son." He undid his seatbelt. "A good son would've come home more than once every few years."

"Hey, now. Don't talk about the man I love that way." I picked my purse up from the floorboard. "Besides, you have your reasons. Don't forget that."

Reasons like getting kicked out of the house when he was sixteen because he wanted to marry his high school sweetheart. Ezra had made a life-altering choice when he decided to have unprotected sex with Kati. And then another life-altering choice when he decided he wanted to be a husband and a father. His parents hadn't been able to fully get behind his decisions, and because of this, they lost out on having a close relationship with their son as he became an adult. Don't get me wrong, I understood how hard it must've been for them, watching their son go down a road that they thought would be a lifetime commitment to heartbreak and failure. I'm sure they thought he had ruined his future. Maybe they still did. I had no idea how much of his successes he shared with them.

I got out of the car and waited for Ezra to come around from his side before we walked together to the door. There was a pine wreath decorated with red and green glass bulbs, pinecones, and a sign hanging in the center that spelled out, The Holdens. I'll admit, I was a jumble of nerves. Or, as my grandmother would say, nervous as a cat in a room full of rocking chairs.

Would they dislike me? Probably. Did I care? More than I should.

I straightened my coat and finger-combed the ends of my hair as we went up the concrete steps. I waited anxiously for Ezra to ring the doorbell.

There hadn't been a need. The door opened. A woman with gray-streaked dark hair that was pulled back in a loose bun and wearing pale blue sweatpants and a matching sweatshirt stood in the opening. Her gray-green hazel eyes weren't the same color as Ezra's, but there was a similar shape to them, and her brows arched the same way his did when he was surprised.

She glanced at me and made an effort to fix her hair as she turned her gaze back to him. "I thought you were coming around two-thirty."

"Hi, Mom," he said. "Do you want me to come back?"

The lines around her eyes deepened then softened as I'm sure a million thoughts raced through her mind. "No, of course not. I want you to stay. I'm just surprised, is all." She smiled warmly at him and then looked at me again. "You must be Nora."

*I must be,* I thought to myself. But aloud, I said, "And you must be Lynn. It's so nice to meet you."

"You as well." She stepped back from the entryway. "Well, come on in before we let out all the heat. Don't mind the mess. I've been doing some cookie baking today, and I haven't had a chance to straighten up yet."

The floors were dark hardwood and looked original. The walls were a light buttery yellow with white accents everywhere, including some ornately carved cornices and all the molding. A seven-foot Christmas tree stood in the back corner of the living room, stacked high with presents around the base. It had red and green ribbons hanging down the sides and a lit star at the top. There was an oversized brown couch, a matching loveseat and recliner, a dark wood coffee table and two end tables with lamps. Other furniture was laced with faux-pine garland and candles, and the walls were lit up with colorful lights. There had been a real effort to create Christmas cheer.

The only mess I could detect was a rumpled red, green, and white afghan on the couch, along with red and green throw pillows that had been bunched to one side. There was a doll and a plushie raccoon on a cushion, and the coffee table had two half-full mugs of what looked like hot cocoa and a plate with crumbs on it.

"My grandbabies." Lynn smiled. "Elaine took them out for some shopping and lunch to get them out of the house for a while." She picked up the mugs and the plate.

The aroma of apple pie lightly scented the room. It had to be from a good quality candle or room freshener because it lacked the warmth of freshly baked apple pie. Still, it was enough to bring up a memory.

*"Easy-peasy, get your fingers out of that pie tin," a woman says with a giggle. She smacks the young boy's hand.*

*The boy, who is almost as tall as the woman, pulls his hand back and sticks his finger in his mouth to lick off the filling, then laughs as he pokes his finger into the latticed crust again. The woman chases him around a butcher block-topped island.*

*"I'm going to tan your hide," she says playfully and without conviction. The boy makes a triumphant noise as he runs out of the kitchen.*

*The woman sighs happily as she picks up a piece of broken crust from near the pie.*

*A tall man comes into the kitchen. "Where's Ezra?"*

*"Hiding," she tells him. "Gosh, he's getting so tall. Pretty soon, he'll outgrow me."*

*The man pulls the woman into his arms and kisses her. "He'll never outgrow you."*

I slowly let out a breath as the memory dissipated. Ezra had been too busy looking around to notice that I'd blanked for a moment. Good. This bittersweet memory was not his, and his mother had a right to her own private thoughts.

"Where's dad?" Ezra asked.

"He went over to your Aunt Lettie's to grab some extra plates and silverware for Christmas day."

Ezra shook his head. "You should've just picked up some paper plates and plastic forks. No one would've cared."

She gave him a stern look. "I would've cared."

The first time I met Ezra, I'd been making jasmine-scented soaps, and it had triggered a memory for him of his mother arranging jasmine flowers. She'd hugged and kissed him and called him Easy-peasy. The love between them had been so natural and relaxed.

Not like now. The tension was thick enough to cut with a carving knife.

"Can I do anything to help?" I asked. "I'm not a great cook, but I wash a mean dish."

Lynn gave me a slight wave at her hip. "You're my guest," she said. "Guests don't do the clean-up."

"Fair." I took my jacket off and automatically took

Ezra's from him when he did the same. "Where can I put these?"

"There are some hooks by the front door." Lynn tugged at the ribbed hem of her sweatshirt. "I'll be right back."

As I took the coats to the hooks, his mother walked through an arch on the other side of the living room and disappeared.

Ezra followed me. "This is weird, right?"

"A little," I agreed. "But we surprised her. I'm sure she's dealing with a lot right now between the holidays and your dad's illness." Whatever it was. "Hey, he's healthy enough to drive. That's a good sign, right?"

He chewed his lower lip for a moment, then wrapped his arms around me. "We'll see."

I hugged him back, and I could feel all the rigidity of tension in his shoulders. It made me wish I had magical words of wisdom to help.

"Why don't you two come back to the kitchen for some coffee or tea?" Lynn asked as she came back into the living room with her hair neatly combed back. I was sorry we'd surprised her. Unexpected company when you weren't ready could feel a bit like an ambush.

I stepped out of Ezra's arms and gave her a warm smile. "Some tea sounds nice."

"Bathroom first," Ezra said.

"It hasn't moved since the last time you were here," his mom replied. To me, she beckoned, "Come on."

The kitchen, also decorated with garland, lights, and other Christmas adornments, had a mobile chalk-green center island with a butcher block top. The same one from the memory. I placed my hand on the surface, aware that there was a lot of history in this room. Dark blue shaker-style cabinets and white countertops, covered with a dozen tins that were filled with a variety of cookies, worked as a complementary contrast. The floors were the same hardwood as the living room. The white appliances were clean with signs of wear. Older, but treated with care. I smiled. The same could be said about me. The oven was cracked open, and there was a concentration of heat around it. The large double sink had four baking sheets stacked vertically inside the left one.

Lynn filled an electric kettle with water from the right side of the sink and plugged it into an outlet near a four-toast toaster. "You want hot tea, right?"

I nodded. "Definitely."

She took a box from a drawer under the counter and put it on the center island. It was a variety sample box of specialty teas. She gave me an almost embarrassed grin. "I don't have a lot of call to use these. They were a gift from a friend. Pick your poison."

I recognized the brand. "The oolong is really good," I remarked. "I'll take that one."

"I think I'll do the green jasmine." She plucked both out of the box, set them on the counter, then closed the box and put it back in the drawer. "It won't take long. The kettle is fast. My sister, Lettie, and her husband,

Orsen, went to England a couple years ago for their anniversary. The first thing she did when she got home was order us both an electric kettle. She said everyone has them over there. It's life changing."

"I have one, too," I told her. "I love it. I use it to boil water for my oatmeal."

She grinned, and it lit up her whole face. "I do the same thing. Tea and breakfast without dirtying a pot."

"I wouldn't dirty a pot without the kettle."

"Oh," Her eyes widened. "You don't cook."

"Not if I can help it." I waved off the idea. "Ezra's a pretty good cook, though."

Lynn shook her head. "Hal can't boil water to save his life."

Lynn snickered, her humor genuine and warm. It was hard to reconcile Ezra's image of his inflexible, controlling mother and the woman making me tea.

"Good thing you have the kettle, then." I snorted at my own stupid joke. Since Lynn brought up Hal, I used the opening to snoop. "Ezra tells me that his dad and Uncle Orsen dress as Santa every year for the walk. Are they doing it this year?" It stood to reason that if Hal was sick, he might not be physically able to do the parade.

Her gaze went to the counter. She dusted a crumb onto the floor, then pushed a loose strand of hair behind her ear. "I don't think I could talk him out of it, even if I wanted to."

I hadn't meant to upset her. "Are you okay?"

"Yes." She waved off my concern and forced a smile. "Ezra must be setting up camp in there."

Ezra had been in the bathroom for a while. I glanced toward the arch.

Lynn gave me a conspiratorial look, and she whispered, "When he was a boy, the first thing he'd do when he came home from school was go and poop. I think there's something about our threshold that has a laxative effect on him."

My mouth dropped open in stunned silence, and then I hooted a laugh. Lynn started laughing with me.

*Honk, honk, honk* a car horn blared. Lynn's face fell again, and her laughter dried up. "That'll be Hal. He's going to need help bringing stuff in."

"Then we better help," Ezra said from the archway. He had his cop face on, the one he used when he was following evidence. I was beginning to suspect he'd been doing more snooping than pooping in the bathroom.

# CHAPTER
# FOUR

Hal Holden stood by the open passenger side door of his blue 1990 GMC pickup truck as he tugged on a box in the seat. He was a couple inches taller than Ezra but with the same deep-set eyes, high cheekbones, and wide mouth. There was no denying they were father and son.

"Hal," Lynn scolded. "Leave it."

The man pulled his shoulders back and huffed, "I'm not an invalid," as he turned to face her. His irritation turned to happily surprised when he spied Ezra. "Hey, stranger. Good to see you." He took a wobbly step toward his son and held out his hand. "I thought you weren't going to be here for a few more hours."

"Hey, Dad." They shook hands. "We decided to pop over before checking in at Thorny Creek." He shook his head at the truck. "I can't believe you're still driving that old beater."

"I just had the engine rebuilt two years ago. She's practically brand new." Hal looked at my car. "Don't tell me you're buying foreign these days."

"No, my Chevy is back home." Ezra gestured to my mini-SUV with a quick jerk of his thumb. "We brought Nora's car because it has more room for bags and stuff in the back."

"And it's more comfortable for long drives." I smiled at Hal. "Hi, I'm the aforementioned Nora."

"Call me Hal." Hal leaned toward me, and I shook his hand. "Glad to finally meet you, Nora."

I stepped back to give Ezra and his dad some room.

Lynn skirted around Hal and got the box out of the passenger seat while the man was distracted by his son. It was too cold to be outside without my coat on, but there had been an urgency in her action to get outside before Hal could carry anything in, so Ezra and I had followed her without donning our jackets.

"Anything else need grabbing?" I asked her.

"There's a bag on the floor there." She pointed to a cute cloth tote covered in pictures of Christmas trees and presents. "It's got the silverware and some odds and ends that I wanted."

When I leaned over to grab it, a brisk breeze went right up the back of my sweater. "Woo, cold," I muttered as I hurriedly snatched the woven handles and lifted them out. It was half full of red cloth napkins along with some candles, a bundle of forks, knives, and spoons. The silverware gave the tote heft.

Swiftly, I followed Lynn back into the house, leaving the two Holden men chatting in the cold driveway.

The box of dishes clattered as she set it down on the center island. "Here." She indicated the space next to the box for me to put the tote. "It's feeling a lot like snow," the woman observed.

"The humidity is making everything damp, and they're calling for a cold front," I agreed. I plopped the bag onto the surface. "We might just get a white Christmas."

"They're overrated," she said, then gave me a sly grin. "Do I sound Grinchy?"

"Only a smidge." I giggled. "The house is full of holiday cheer, and you baked an awful lot of cookies."

"I make them for everyone in the family. It's a cheap Christmas gift."

"Are you kidding? When you factor in labor, each one of those tins is worth at least twenty-five dollars. That's a substantial present."

She frowned as she scanned the counter of tins, then nodded. "You know what? You're absolutely right." The kettle we'd abandoned roared to boiling. Lynn widened her eyes. "The water's ready."

We decided to make up four cups of tea. Lynn opened the drawer and picked English Breakfast for Ezra and Dragon Well green tea for Hal. Ezra was more of a coffee drinker, so English Breakfast, being a stronger black tea, was a good choice. Soon, the four of us were settled into the living room.

"Did you all have a nice drive in?" Hal's eyes lit up when he smiled. I was once again reminded of Ezra.

"Yep. Roads weren't too busy," Ezra answered.

"We stopped at Weston's Restaurant for lunch," I added.

"They have the best onion rings," Lynn remarked. "Gosh, Hal, we haven't eaten there in a while."

He smiled at his wife. "We should make a plan."

She looked startled for a moment, then narrowed her gaze on him. "We'll see."

Ezra took the opportunity to transition the conversation. "While we were at the restaurant, we ran into Penny. What's she been up to lately?"

"You didn't ask her?"

He shifted uncomfortably under his mom's scrutiny. "Our interaction was brief."

I arched a brow at him.

He shrugged. "Anyways, I was just wondering how she's been doing. She seemed a little on edge."

It wasn't the smoothest of segues, but I gave him an E for effort.

Hal took a sip of his tea. He made a face at the beverage and then looked at Ezra. "She got laid off from her secretarial job at Mega-Shield Insurance and has been working in the front office at Pike Manufacturing for about a year."

"Hal put in a good word for her," Lynn said, "He's the day shift supervisor over the fabrication department now."

"Congrats on the promotion, Dad," Ezra said. "That's great. You deserve it."

"Hal's been at the plant now, for what, Thirty-six years?" Lynn interjected.

Hal nodded, looking pleased by the opportunity to talk about his work. "Yep. It's been thirty-six years. I know every job out on the factory floor backward and forward. I started working there when Lynn was pregnant with Ezra. Worked my way up from the line." He shrugged. "Even so, I don't see Penny much at the plant. The last I heard, she was doing a good job, but that was the first couple of months she was there."

Lynn set her teacup down on the coffee table. "Lettie says that Penny's been helping Clark Faber organize the Santa Walk."

Ezra cocked a brow. "Clark Faber?"

"He's a Springfield local who just moved to Hillside this past year after he retired from the air force," Hal said. "Pike hired him as the new human resource manager back in June after Dale Watkin left. Penny's his assistant."

"Clark decided to retire after his mother got sick. She suffered from Alzheimer's, so he moved back to the area to be close to her. A good son." Lynn sighed. "She died a few months ago."

I didn't think that was a dig at Ezra, but I'd have to understand the family dynamic better before I could make that call. Even so, I saw the wounding on Ezra's face.

Hal, oblivious to the shift in the room between mother and son, gave a condolent nod. "From what I heard, Penny stepped up to help him when he had to settle his mother's affairs."

"Lettie says Penny's really turning her life around," Lynn added as if she needed to defend her niece.

A grunt of disbelief escaped Ezra.

His mom's brows dipped at him. "You have something to say?"

Ezra hemmed for a moment, then dropped the bomb. "She was meeting Rob."

"Really?" Lynn frowned. "Elaine's Rob?"

Ezra nodded. "Yep."

"Penny's family." His mom pished. "I'm sure it wasn't anything."

Hal harrumphed. "I knew he was cheating on Elaine. She wouldn't say, but this seems like proof."

"That's not proof," Lynn said firmly. "If he was stepping out on her, she would've told me."

Hal flexed his fingers and rubbed the knees of his jeans. "The next time I see him...."

"Hopefully, we won't run into him any time soon." Lynn returned her attention to Ezra and changed the subject to a happier topic. "How's Mason?"

"Good." Ezra's chest puffed with pride. "He's a senior at MU." MU was the University of Missouri in Columbia. Mason was studying biomedical science there.

Hal held up a finger to indicate number one and wagged it at us. "Go, Tigers."

Ezra beamed with pleasure. "He made the Dean's list last semester."

"Didn't he just graduate last year?" Lynn asked.

"Yep," Ezra replied warmly. "But he earned his associate degree by taking college courses while he was in high school."

Ezra's dad reached out and gave him a congratulatory pat on the knee. "He gets his smarts from you."

Ezra half smiled. "I'm afraid Mason far surpasses me in the brains department."

"He and my goddaughter Ari were part of the STEM program back home," I said.

"What's that?" Lynn asked.

"Science, technology, engineering, and mathematics," I answered. "They were both in the program at Garden Cove High School."

"They build robots and other really cool things," Ezra added.

"Is that how you two met?" Lynn asked. "Through the kids?"

"No, nothing that simple." I glanced over at Ezra, and he was looking at me with a light in his eyes that made my heart skip a beat. "He arrested my best friend for murder."

Lynn's eyes widened in shock. "You're kidding me."

"Not in the least." I shook my head.

"And not exactly accurate." The smile on Ezra's face

was worth every bit of this rehashing. "We actually met when I served her with a restraining order."

"For what?" Hal said. He and Lynn leaned forward, eager to hear the story.

"She pulled a gun on a man...."

"Who was stalking my best friend," I emphasized so I didn't sound like a crazed killer. "And he'd shown up at my house trying to track her down."

"What happened to him?" Lynn asked.

"He's the guy my friend was arrested for murdering."

The woman stirred her tea with her fingertip, captivated by the tale. "But she didn't do it."

"No way. Gilly, while having a decent motive, was completely innocent." I turned my gaze to Ezra. "Your son helped me prove it."

"Don't you mean you helped me?" He playfully nudged me with his elbow but addressed his parents. "Nora is quite the detective. She's consulted with the police department on several investigations."

"Really?" Lynn asked. "How did you get involved in consulting?"

"My dad was the chief of police until he died, and my ex is the current chief of police in Garden Cove. However, it wasn't a career I was ever interested in. But in the past couple of years, since my best friend's case, I've developed a gift for sniffing out crime."

Ezra snorted a loud laugh. "That's right on the nose," he teased.

I rolled my eyes and turned my attention to his

parents. "Did you want to see some pictures of Mason? I took them this summer when he was home for break."

"Oh, yes," Lynn exclaimed. "I haven't seen Mason since Kati moved him away."

That was nine years ago. Wow. That was a long time not to see their grandchild. I retrieved my phone from my purse, and I saw I had several missed texts and phone calls from Gilly, but I didn't immediately check them. If the shop had burned down since this morning, I could wait a little while longer to find out.

First pictures.

I tapped the picture folder and scrolled through until I found the ones with Mason in them. I pulled up the first one I landed on. Mason and Ari, Gilly's daughter, were posing playfully, and the lake was in the background.

I handed the phone to Lynn. "We had a barbeque at Ezra's cabin. I took that picture down by the dock."

"You have a cabin on the lake?" Hal asked.

My gut squeezed as Ezra gave them a crisp "Yep." The conversation up to this point had been so pleasant I'd almost forgotten they were estranged.

Lynn had grown quiet. Finally, she commented, "He looks just like you did at that age."

"He is definitely a mini-Ezra," I agreed.

She handed the phone back to me. "Pretty girl. Ari, you say? Is she Mason's girlfriend?"

"They're just friends." Ari had strongly hinted that Mason was gay, but until he was ready to tell people, I wasn't about to *out* the kid to his dad or his grand-parents.

"I wish you would've brought him to Hillside for the Holiday," Lynn said wistfully. "We would love to see him more than once every decade."

Ezra arched his brow at his mom. "The road from Garden Cove to Hillside goes both ways. You all could always come and visit."

Lynn's shoulders bunched, and her expression cooled. "We've never been invited."

I shifted uncomfortably as the mood in the room altered.

"You don't need an invitation to visit family," Ezra countered.

"Apparently, you do," his mom argued. "Would you ever have come home if I hadn't asked?"

"Now, Lynn," Hal cautioned.

Ezra's ears were turning an unflattering shade of red, but he spoke calmly. "I'm here now."

Whoa. Things had gotten super tense. I thought the room needed a moment to breathe. I certainly did. I stood up from the couch. "We have got a bunch of presents for the tree," I chimed in. "Might as well get it done sooner rather than later. Ezra, you want to give me a hand?"

He got to his feet beside me. "Good idea." To his parents, he said, "Then we better go get checked in at the B and B."

His mom sighed. "I'm sorry. I'm not trying to fight with you."

Ezra nodded. "I'm not trying to fight with you either."

She gave him a tight smile. "Good. Then we won't fight."

"That'd be a first," Hal muttered.

Lynn gave him a warning glare, and I fought down a nervous titter.

Ezra headed out. Lynn touched my arm to stop me from leaving after him.

"I'm so sorry," she said. "This isn't the first impression I wanted to make."

"It's fine." I had real sympathy for her. Whatever she was going through with her husband couldn't be easy. Add to that a rift with her son, and I imagined she was struggling to cope with it all. "Family is messy."

"That's the truth." The tension around her mouth and eyes eased. "Do you want some help bringing stuff inside?"

"No, we have it."

She stared toward the door where Ezra had exited. "I'm sure things will be less tense this afternoon."

I didn't think anything would change between then and now, but I liked her optimism.

I t didn't take long to get to Thorny Creek Inn from Ezra's parents' house. The estate was less than a mile out of town, and the gated, tree-lined driveway looked newly paved and immaculately maintained. Ezra's excitement might have been dampened by our afternoon with his folks, but upon seeing the manor at the end of the drive, his eyes lit up.

"Wowza," I said, impressed. The expansive Queen Anne-style three-story house was light salmon pink with white trim. "This place is right out of a Jane Austen novel." It also had a partial wrap-around covered porch, along with a wrapped second-story covered balcony. Some of the windows were stained glass with floral designs. It had a round turret on the left side that ended in a steep-pitched roof framed by an ornate gable that gave the place a slightly gothic vibe. "This is so freaking cool."

"Right?" Ezra grabbed our luggage from the back. "I told you."

"It's amazing. Nothing like I was imagining."

"What had you imagined?"

I grabbed my carry-on out of the backseat. "Oh, I don't know. Something more rustic, like a barnyard house with a rodeo theme."

"Ha," he said. "Let's get checked in. We might have just enough time before the Santa parade for a bull ride." He wiggled his brows at me.

I choked on a laugh and shook my head. I smacked him on the butt as he walked past me. "Get a long little doggie." My phone beeped. Shoot. I'd forgotten about the missed texts I got earlier. "Hey, I'll meet you inside. I want to check in with Gilly."

"Take your time." Ezra winked at me. "But not too much time."

I was grinning hard enough to make my cheeks hurt when I checked my messages.

> Call me.
>
> Where r u?
>
> Why aren't u calling me?
>
> You better be kidnapped.
>
> Am I going to have to call 911?
>
> You're killing me.
>
> You better be dead.

Don't be dead!

What the actual heck? These were nuclear-threat-level texts. I tapped the green phone in the top corner of the screen to call her. She picked up on the first ring.

"It's about freaking time," she chided.

"Good afternoon to you, too," I replied. "What's so urgent?"

"Scott proposed to me."

"What?" I blinked as the cold air made my eyes water.

"Scott proposed to me," she repeated.

"I...." If Gilly and Scott got married, would Gilly move? I'd bought the house next to her so we could grow old and die together, were all the terrible thoughts that initially went through my brain. I tamped back my fear of losing her and mustered all the enthusiasm she deserved. "Oh my gosh. When? How? What did you say?"

"This morning over breakfast...in bed." She hooted a laugh. "He told me over mimosas and buttery croissants that he's waited his whole life for me. Then he said he hoped I wouldn't make him wait a minute more to spend the rest of my life with him."

"And?"

"And I said yes."

"Congratulations! I'm so happy for you, Gilly. It's wonderful news. Scott's a lucky guy."

"Yeah?"

"You are a freaking catch, baby. You're damn right he's lucky."

She giggled again. "Thanks." After a short pause, she asked, "How's the Holden family reunion going?"

"We stopped over at his parents' place briefly, and it was a little tense but not horrible. We're checking in at the B and B now. Dinner tonight will be the real test."

"You'll keep me up to date?" she asked.

"Only if you text me a picture of the ring."

"I'll do it right now." She sounded so happy. "Hold on. Okay. Yep, that's a good shot. You should be getting it... right now."

My phone dinged. I took it away from my ear and hit my texts. It was a healthy-sized round diamond with a gold pavé band, sparkling with tiny inset diamonds. I put the phone back to my ear. "Amazing and gorgeous, just like you."

"I know, right? Well, I'll let you get back to whatever you were doing."

"I'm going to a rodeo," I half-joked.

Gilly laughed. "Have fun with that."

"Oh, I am planning on it." I hung up with a smile on my face.

The inside of the B&B was just as charming as the exterior. A variety of poinsettias, white, pink, and red, were set on end tables, shelves, and other strategic places throughout the large sitting room. A giant nine-foot scotch pine, decorated with gold and silver ornaments and ribbons and topped with a gold star, was next to an archway leading to a dining room. There was a large rectangular table with a setting for twelve just on the other side. A grand staircase swept up the left side, and the banister was wrapped in pine garland accented with pinecones and holly berries. In other words, the Thorny Creek Inn décor looked as if it had been plucked from the pages of a magazine. Perfectly picturesque.

The scent of cinnamon, orange, and cloves permeated the room.

*"God rest ye, merry gentlemen. Let nothing you dismay,"* a woman with blonde hair sings with an upbeat cadence as she throws cinnamon sticks, orange slices, star anise, and cloves into a pot on the stove. She boops a little girl in a red dress on the nose and continues the song. *"Remember Christ our Savior was born on Christmas Day."*

*She grabs the little girl by the hands, and they dance as she dramatically belts out, "To save my Molly from Satan's lies and when she is led astray. Oh, tidings of comfort and joy. Comfort and joy. Oh-oooooh, tidings of comfort and joy."*

The lovely aroma and memory warmed me. Well, that and the heat from the electric fireplace on the other side of the arch. One of the few modern touches, I noted, but its elegant dark wood surrounded with carved cornices and a thick mantle kept it from looking out of place. The whole thing was almost enough to take my mind off Gilly's engagement. Almost.

I was happy for my best friend. Scott Graham, a local doctor, was so good to her and for her. They'd been dating for a year now, which at a certain age, stops being a short amount of time, so it wasn't as if they were rushing into things. He would treat her like a queen, of that I had no doubt. And she deserved all the happiness coming her way. But knowing this didn't ease the anxiety squeezing my guts.

A tall woman in her sixties with short, dark gray hair was handing Ezra a packet. I forced myself out of the future and into the present to join them.

"I'm Molly Higgins," the woman announced. "Owner of Thorny Creek Inn. Third generation."

"Tidings of comfort and joy," I muttered, remembering the Molly lyric in the memory.

"What?" Molly asked with a look of curious surprise.

"This inn is so full of comfort and joy," I amended, then introduced myself. "I'm Nora Black, and all I can say is, wow. This place is right out of a fairy tale."

"But without the villains," Molly laughed. "You two are so welcome, and I hope we can make your holiday merry and bright." She wore a white sweater with red poinsettias on the front, and her shoulders were pulled back with pride. "Your keys, the menu, the property map, and the wifi password are all in the envelope. You can get new towels from the linen closet if you need them. Housekeeping is available tomorrow, but not on Christmas," she said. "I'll be hosting a Christmas dinner for our guests that afternoon, but I see you checked "no" on the RSVP. We have six other guests, almost a full house, so if you change your mind, let me know. Two more plates won't make a difference."

"Thank you, ma'am." Ezra rubbed the hinge of his jaw. "We'll be eating with my family on Christmas, but I appreciate the offer."

As we followed Molly through a long hallway, a mistletoe hung from one of the many arches.

Ezra stopped me for a kiss. "It's tradition."

"Who am I to buck tradition?" I went up on my tiptoes to meet his lips for a quick peck.

Molly waited for us at the back door. "The carriage house is down the bricked path past the veranda and the garden. The entryway is a staircase on the left side."

I widened my eyes at Ezra. "The carriage house?"

"Just wait," he said. He nodded to Molly. "Thank you."

She smiled. "If you folks need anything at all, my cellphone number is in the packet as well."

Ezra gave me a warm look. "I brought everything I need.

"Great," Molly responded enthusiastically. "But just in case you forgot a toothbrush or whatever." She held the door open for us. "The meal schedule is in there as well. Breakfast is served at nine sharp in the morning."

"Sounds good." I was a morning person, so I was going to be up much earlier than nine. "Is there coffee in the room?"

"The carriage house is our deluxe suite, and it has a mini-kitchen equipped with a single-serve coffee maker, along with coffee and tea pods. Sugar, sweetener, and creamer are on the coffee bar as well," Molly said, preening with pride.

"Perfect." I brushed my shoulder against Ezra's arm. "It's all perfect."

"Wait until you see the view," Molly added when we got out onto the large half-octagon-shaped veranda. "The lake is stunning from your balcony."

I'll admit, Ezra's excitement for the place was starting to feel contagious. I was practically bouncing on my toes as we made our way down the brick path past a tall garden shed covered in ivy vines that had mostly lost their leaves. Boughs of pine and holly on stakes lined the well-maintained pathway, interspersed with manicured evergreens that were wrapped in holiday lights. They weren't on now while it was still light out, but it would be dark before we left for dinner. I was eager to see the place in all its Christmas glory.

"How are you feeling?" I asked Ezra. "You know, after the incident with your mom."

"Incident?" he asked with nonchalance. "I don't recall any incident."

I gave him a side-eyed glance. "Whatever you want to call it. Things got a little intense."

He shrugged. "She knows how to push my buttons."

"First, let me say this. I am one hundred percent on your side, no matter what."

"Good to know."

"However, do you think maybe the button-pushing might be an inherited talent?"

"Hah," he said without humor.

He hadn't asked his parents about Hal being sick, but I could tell he'd found out something when he'd left Lynn and me alone in the kitchen. "What did you find in the bathroom?" I asked. "Did you find out something about your dad's illness?"

"A blood thinner and pain pills."

"Huh." My mother had been on blood thinners and pain pills early on in her cancer treatment. Toward the end, it had been just the pain medicine. "Did you find any other medications?"

"No." He shook his head. "There was a box of sterile bandages and some wound cleaning supplies."

"Hmmmm." I would have expected antinausea medications and a few medications with unpronounceable names. "What do you think it is?'

"I haven't a clue." Soon, we came upon a small two-story building, baby blue with white trim, with two rustic bay doors and farmhouse windows up top. He shook the melancholy from his expression. "We're here."

I was suddenly nostalgic for my mother. Not surprising, considering the holiday. But I think some of that nostalgia was Gilly-related. I liked to think of myself as someone who went with the flow, but honestly, I wasn't ready for any more big changes. Luckily for Gilly, her decisions weren't about me.

Ezra lifted both suitcases and carried them up the steps. He set them down on the stoop, then took the envelope from his jacket and retrieved the door key.

He unlocked the door, but before going inside, he asked, "Is something bugging you?"

"No." I sighed. "Yes."

He opened the door and put the bags inside. "Is it my mom? Did she say something to you?"

"Your mom was fine. Lovely even."

He held the door open for me, and I went inside. My eyes widened as I took in the suite. It had a vaulted white tongue and groove ceiling and a saddle oak hardwood floor. The king-sized bed with a lush, crisply white down comforter and a ton of cozy pillows with blue, pale pink, and butter accents were against the far wall. There were two cushioned rockers with an end table between them in front of sliding glass doors that opened to a balcony overlooking the lake. A claw-footed bathtub big enough for two people was on a tiled floor with an oval curtain hanger hanging above it for some privacy. Thankfully, the toilet, vanity, and shower were tucked privately away with an actual door. There was a bar set up with a fridge, a microwave, and, as promised, a single-cup coffee maker with an assortment of coffees and teas. They'd even put a bistro table with two chairs in the area. There was a gift basket on the table with an assortment of fruits, cookies, and candies, along with a bottle of wine and a vase with a dozen snow-white roses.

"Wow. I know I'm saying that a lot, but... wow. Holy cow." I turned into Ezra's arms and slid my hands over his shoulders and behind his neck. "This place is amazing."

"You're amazing." He kissed me. "I'm so glad you approve."

"I do indeed." I kissed him back.

"So, what's bugging you?" he asked again.

I stifled a noise of dismay. "Nothing." I didn't want to talk about Gilly's engagement. Not until I had time to get past my unreasonable, selfish motives for not being as happy as I should be for my BFF.

Ezra pressed his forehead to mine. "Come on. Spill."

My frown deepened. "Scott asked Gilly to marry him."

He gave me an amused look. "And you're afraid it's going to give me ideas, huh?"

"What?" I heard the alarm in my voice, so I tried to temper my reaction. "That never crossed my mind."

His chest began to shake with laughter. "I bet it's crossing your mind now."

"Stop it." I gave his chest a playful yet semi-serious slap.

"What? I mean, it's romantic, right? I bring you to my hometown to meet my parents. I arrange for us to stay at an idyllic bed and breakfast in its best suite...."

"Or, instead of this being a romantic getaway, you bring me to a town where no one knows me, and you take me to a secluded inn out in the middle of nowhere, put us in the room farthest away from the main house so no one can hear my screams when you try to murder me."

"There would be no try to it," he countered. "If I was going to murder you, I'd make sure I could get it done."

"Nice. You wish. I've been taking self-defense classes with Reese, and I'm pretty sure I could hold my own."

"I know of more than one or two killers who would agree with you."

"Keep that in mind." I had managed to fight off some dangerous individuals in the past. My survival mode was strong.

Ezra dipped his head, and his lips seared mine in a toe-curling kiss that made me swoon.

I slipped my hands over his superiorly firm butt. "Is it just me, or is it getting hot in here?"

"It's not just you." He stepped back and unzipped my winter coat, slipping it over my shoulders and down my back. He walked me backward until my calves touched the bed and then, to my delight, proceeded to take his clothes off.

"Wooo-wee." I stripped off my sweater and undid my jeans. "This is turning into my kind of holiday."

Ezra grinned and gave me his best John McLane impression from his favorite Christmas movie, *Die Hard*. "Welcome to the party, Pal."

I whooped with laughter when he wrapped his arms around me, and we tumbled onto the bed. "Yippee kai-yay."

CHAPTER

# SIX

The streets of downtown Hillside were a sea of red and white as Santas from all walks of life paraded past happy families who cheered them on from the sidewalks. Christmas music blared over loudspeakers. I cracked up when "Grandma Got Run Over By A Reindeer" started, and a group of six people, one Santa, four reindeer, and one person in a frumpy house gown and gray wig, reenacted the song for the crowd.

Ezra's smile was as big as mine.

A couple strolling past us were eating candied pecans from a paper cone.

I tugged on Ezra's arm. "Ooo! Let's go get some nuts."

The cinnamon-roasted candied pecans reminded me of my childhood. My father would buy them for me at the fair every year. He liked the pecans best because he said, "they don't break my teeth like the almonds."

I used to think it was a cautionary tale because he had a partial denture for his two front teeth. It was only after I got older that I found out that he'd been assaulted while on duty, and his teeth had been broken during the struggle. He'd spun the tale to make his tooth loss less scary for me. Joke was on him. I had a fear of eating almonds for years.

Lynn had called us before we'd left Thorny Creek Inn and told us she and Hal would meet us at the parade. We hadn't been able to find them, but honestly, Ezra wasn't looking that hard.

I underestimated the extent of the variety of food involved in this event. There were food trucks with hot fried apple pies served with vanilla ice cream and warm caramel sauce, loaded baked potatoes, giant cinnamon rolls, and Bavarian pretzels.

"I was thinking way too small with the nuts," I told Ezra.

He chuckled. "We'll get anything you want."

"I knew there was a reason I keep you around."

He hooted a laugh. "I thought it was for my butt."

I looked around, only a little embarrassed that someone might've overheard him, but everyone was too busy watching the spectacle of Santas. I leaned in close to Ezra and smirked, "The butt definitely makes the top five."

He looped his arm across my shoulders. "Top two, at the very least. So, what's it going to be? Fried pies or giant cinnamon rolls?"

"You know me too well." I studied the lines in front of both trucks and decided on the warm dessert with the least amount of people. "Fried apple pie and a hot spiced cider."

His eyes twinkled with mirth. "Good choice."

While we were waiting in line, an air horn blared, and over the loudspeakers, someone said, "Are you all ready for this?" Then a marching band of Santas came around a corner, playing an instrumental of "Let's Get Ready to Rumble" from the movie *Space Jam*. People all around us started dancing and yelling out loud, "Yeah!" when appropriate, as the brass section really took it home.

Ezra grinned. "That's new." He laughed. "Not the song, but the fact that the high school marching band has gotten involved."

I moved my hips back and forth to the beat. "They're great."

A woman dancing in line in front of us said, "They've done it the past couple of years. It's a real hit." She fist-pumped the sky and shouted, "yeah!" with the song.

"This is awesome," I told Ezra. "I've never seen anything like it."

Suddenly distracted, he muttered his acknowledgment. He was staring down the sidewalk, and I picked up on what had drawn his attention. His cousin Penny, dressed in full elf regalia—red tights, green pointed shoes, a long-sleeved green tunic, and a green and red striped hat with a white ball on the end. She seemed to be in a passionate argument with someone dressed in a Santa suit a block down from us. Her hands were expressively telling the not-so-jolly man in a red suit where he could go. Hint: It wasn't the North Pole.

"Maybe I should go check on her," Ezra said.

"You mean snoop?" I asked.

He arched a brow at me. "Exactly."

The pies and cider could wait. "I'm in."

We gave up our places in line and stayed close to the buildings as we made our way toward Penny. Another Santa, who'd had a little too much to drink if I had to guess, staggered up the sidewalk toward us. He bumped into me as he passed by.

"Pardon," he mumbled.

He smelled of peppermint, buttered popcorn, and bourbon. It was a strangely appealing combination, and the aroma triggered my smell-o-vision. We were moving at a quick pace, so I reached out for Ezra to keep from falling as the memory took over.

*"Don't be such a wuss, man. This is the easiest job we'll ever take on," a man says loud enough to be heard at the table over the loud music. He sits in a dark bar in a corner booth with another man. "And the best part," he spreads his hands wide, "there's zero downside."*

*"I don't know," the other man says. He has a John Deere ball cap on. "If we get caught—"*

*"We won't," the lead man reiterates. "Besides, we have someone on the inside." He lifts his drink to the table. "What say you?"*

"*I say, I hope my wife never finds out,*" *the guy in the cap replied.*

"*Whipped!*" *the first guy whooped.*

"*Damn right.*" *He slugged back the drink.* "*Let's do it.*"

When the vision of partying men faded, I found I wasn't holding onto Ezra. Instead, I had grabbed a uniformed officer, who looked completely nonplussed.

My eyes widened. "I'm so sorry."

The cop was a young man, mid-twenties at the most. He had dark hair and brown eyes, and he looked like he was annoyed that he was spending the day babysitting the Santa Walk crowd. "Are you all right, miss?" he asked. "Maybe you should sit down."

"I'm okay," I told him, scanning ahead for Ezra. I saw him closing in on Penny and the disgruntled Claus.

Santa grabbed Penny by the arm, and she jerked away. Ezra was on the bearded jerk, shoving him up against a brick building.

"No, stop!" Penny yelled loud enough I could hear her over the marching band. "Let him go."

The young officer's attention diverted from me to the scene. "Excuse me." He side-stepped me and headed toward the action. I didn't wait for an invitation, and I followed closely after.

The officer, with his taser drawn, ordered Ezra and Santa to put their hands against the wall. Yikes. This was escalating fast.

"This is a misunderstanding," Penny said. "Ezra's my cousin. He thought he was helping."

"This guy was assaulting her," Ezra added, even as he complied with the officer's request to put his hands against the wall.

"He wasn't," Penny disagreed. "I work for him." She threw her hands up in the air. "It wasn't that big of a deal."

"I want to press charges," Boss-man Santa demanded. "He threw me against the wall."

"You grabbed my cousin first," Ezra countered.

"Both of you shut up," the cop ordered.

Oh boy. I held my hands out in a "calm down" manner and said, "I think we all need to take a breath."

The police officer stared at me. "What do you have to do with this?"

I raised my hands defensively. "I'm with the non-Santa." And since Ezra hadn't said it, I added, "He's a police detective."

The officer looked befuddled. "For Hillside?"

"No," Ezra admitted. "I'm just visiting family."

"Let them go, Rogers," a male voice enjoined from behind me. I whipped around. Rob Phillips, the soon-to-be ex-brother-in-law, stood behind me. He waved his hand at the rookie cop. "In the spirit of the holiday."

Officer Rogers' lips thinned with irritation, but then he nodded. "Fine. Stay out of trouble," he told Ezra and the Santa before he rolled his eyes and walked off.

Soon as the policeman was gone, Santa pushed himself away from the wall and stormed off.

"Wait!" Penny hollered after him. Before Ezra could

stop her, she took off down the street in Boss Santa's direction.

"Well, that was a waste of time," Ezra uttered as he watched her go.

Some people don't want saving, I thought. And Penny seemed like one of them.

Ezra glared at Rob. "What do you want?"

I understood his anger. I felt much the same way when Gilly's ex-Gio was caught cheating, and she kicked him out. Frankly, I thought Ezra was being fairly polite.

"Come on, Easy. We used to be friends," Rob cajoled. "Can't we have a civil conversation?"

"You know you hurt my sister," Ezra told him.

Rob spread his hands. "Then you only know half the story."

"You've got to be kidding me." Ezra touched my elbow. "Come on. Let's get that apple pie."

"Ez," Rob said. "Can we talk about it?"

Four guys in full Santa suits, including beards and mustaches, joined us. "Easy, you need some help kicking this guy's ass?" the shortest of the four said. He pulled down his fake white beard and took off his hat. He had reddish-blond hair and deep dimples.

Ezra's expression darkened, then his eyes widened, and he smiled. "Rollo." He shook the man's hand. "It's been a while, bud. How the heck are you doing?"

"Fantastic," Rollo said. "Living the dream."

Rob shook his head and walked off.

Ezra gave a small victory smile and then introduced me to the newcomers. "Nora, this is my cousin Rollo."

"Belonging to your Aunt Lettie and Uncle Orsen," I said.

"Yeah," Rollo chortled. "You're good."

I gave him a quick wink. "That's the word on the streets."

From what Ezra had told me, Rollo was Penny's younger brother. There was another one, even younger, named Baxter.

"These are my buddies Blake, Tom-Tom, and Howdy." He pointed to a tall, lanky fellow, a guy with dark brown hair, an upturned nose that made him look a little piggish, and a waist tire, and finally, a guy with dark hair and eyes, a narrow face and an aquiline nose, the combo making him look Mediterranean.

"Howdy," I greeted, unable to help myself. I grimaced. "Sorry. It's been a weird day, and I'm feeling a little punchy."

"I get it all the time." Howdy smiled and inclined his head to me. "I don't mind."

I could smell the bourbon mint combo again. "What is that scent?" I asked. "It smells like someone got popcorn and a candy cane drunk."

Tom-Tom pointed at a stand not too far from us. "That's crazy accurate," he said. "Candy cane popcorn balls with a bourbon butter glaze. It tastes as good as it smells."

"Thanks, Tom-Tom." The man gave me a smile and a

thumbs-up. In my head, I was figuring out how to turn the aroma combo into a soap for my shop.

"Hoo boy," Rollo groaned. "There's our dads." He pointed in the direction of the street and laughed. "You have to admire their willingness to make fools of themselves every year."

We'd seen a hundred-plus Santas of every variation. I wasn't sure what the dads could do that was so embarrassing.

Ezra's chin tucked, and he choked on a laugh. "Why is my dad green and Uncle Orsen yellow?"

I could answer the green one. "Your dad is the Grinch that stole Christmas," I said. "See, he has hair coming off his green gloves. Hilarious."

Ezra looked unconvinced. "And Uncle Orsen?"

Rollo supplied the answer. "Homer Simpson. The episode where Homer takes a job as a mall Santa."

I'd never watched the Simpsons, but I would've had to have been born under a rock not to know about the cartoon. The green and yellow Santas waved when they passed by us. We all waved back.

"We better go," Rollo said. "We're part of the Grand Marshall escort."

"See you at dinner tonight," Ezra told him. After the four men left, Ezra nudged me. "Pie?" he asked.

"Definitely."

# CHAPTER
# SEVEN

Oriental Palace Buffet was in the Hillside Shopping Center, a strip mall on the east side of town near the highway exit. It was situated between a Snip N Clip and a pawn shop. The fragrance of garlic, sesame oil, onions, roasting meats, and vegetables set off a series of memories but nothing noteworthy or exciting.

It was a little after seven o'clock, but between lunch and the Santa Walk fried apple pie and vanilla ice cream, which, for the record, had been delicious, I was still full.

The hostess, an Asian woman, escorted us past four buffet lines of food and two rows of booths before we took a right near the bathrooms and into a banquet room. Inside, there was a long table with at least eighteen people, including three small children.

My heart fluttered as most of the heads swiveled in our direction.

"Ezra!" a large man with a gray beard, black mustache, and a balding head shouted. I recognized him, even without yellow makeup, as the Homer Simpson Santa. He stood up and shoved his meaty palm at Ezra. "It's good to see you."

"Good to see you, Uncle Orsen." Ezra obliged the man with a friendly handshake.

I was beginning to think this was not a family of huggers until a red-haired woman next to Uncle Orsen grabbed Ezra into an embrace.

"It's been too long," she said. "You don't write. You don't call."

Ezra smiled at me over her shoulder. "Hey, Aunt Lettie. Merry Christmas."

"You're the best present." She squeezed him tighter for a moment, then gave his back a slap. "I'm so happy you decided to come home this year." Aunt Lettie pushed him an arms-length away. "I swear you get more handsome every time I see you."

Ezra put his hand on my back. "Aunt Lettie and Uncle Orsen, this is my partner, Nora Black."

Orsen gave me a strange look. "Work partner?"

Ezra shook his head and put his arm around my shoulder. "More like life."

"Oh," Orsen said. "She's your sweetheart."

"Sure," Ezra agreed with a grin. "That's accurate, too."

"Interesting," Lettie added, giving Lynn a quick glance. "How long have you two been…. You know."

"Together?" Ezra asked. He pivoted his gaze to mine, and he smiled. "How long has it been now? Three years?"

"Just about," I agreed. It had been two years, seven months, and some change, but I didn't want to sound as if I were counting the days.

"It's nice to meet you, Nora," Orsen wiped his hand on his shirt and then offered it to me. "Any friend of Ezra's is welcome at the family table."

I shook his hand. "Nice to meet you too."

Ezra's dad beamed with pleasure as everyone got up from the table to greet Ezra and me, while his mom's face was fixed with a tight-lipped smile.

Introductions went around the table. There was Rollo, who I'd met earlier, and his brother Baxter, along with their wives, Carla and Wendy. Lettie was Lynn's younger sister, and there was another sister, Lorena, the oldest, and her daughter Rose Marie. Rose Marie was in her mid-forties, and she had her adult son, Ryan, with her, along with Ryan's girlfriend Amber and their toddler son Dusty.

Lastly, a brunette in a Christmas sweater, who was sitting with two small children on either side of her, got up and hugged Ezra. "How's it going, brother?"

"Good, you?" Ezra gave her a sympathetic look.

"I'm surviving," she said, then looked over at two little girls, both in booster seats. "You know how it goes."

"I do," he affirmed. He turned to me. "Nora, this is my sister Elaine. Elaine, this is...."

"The notorious Nora Black." She had her arms crossed over her chest as she sized me up with a sweeping gaze from head to toe. Finally, she shook her head and grinned. "You weren't lying. She's very pretty."

"I never lie," Ezra quipped.

Elaine's eyes, the same color of blue as Hal's, met mine. "Then you must be the smartest, most talented woman on the face of the earth," she teased.

I rolled my eyes but laughed. "That sounds slightly exaggerated."

"Not an exaggeration," Ezra smirked. "Even so, I don't think I said all that. At least, not out loud."

"Not in so many words." Elaine shrugged. "But you definitely implied."

There was an easiness between them that reminded me of Gilly and me. I found myself really liking Elaine. "It's so nice to finally meet you," I told her.

Two small girls, one around five, the other around two, closed in on Elaine's legs. "This is Prissy." She caressed the back of the older girl's neck. "And this bashful thing," she picked up the small one, "is Tessa." She smiled at her daughters. "Girls, this is your Uncle Easy."

Ezra's eyes softened at the corners. "You need to send updated pictures. They have gotten so big."

Elaine shook her head. "That happens when you don't see a child but once every few years."

Two waitresses came to the table with trays filled with drinks and began handing them out.

"I think we're all here." Orsen spread his hands wide. "We should go get our food."

"What about Penny?" Rollo asked. "She's not here yet."

Lettie fretted nervously, "I haven't been able to get a hold of her since this afternoon. She told me last week she was planning on coming, but you know how she is."

Orsen nodded. "She's probably finishing up stuff for the Santa Walk. I'm sure she'll get here when she can." He didn't sound certain, but even so, he pulled his shoulders back and lifted his head. "She helped organize the whole thing this year."

Lettie gave her husband a grateful smile. "This was the biggest turnout yet."

Ezra gripped my hand and leaned to my ear. "If we're lucky, she'll be busy all night," he whispered.

"So, Nora," Lorena, the oldest aunt, said on approach. "I hear you own a shop. What do you all sell?"

"Hand-crafted soaps and lotions, along with skin and hair care."

Her nose wrinkled as if she were smelling something unpleasant. "You make your own products?"

"Most of them," I told her. "It's always been a dream of mine."

Lorena crossed her arms over her chest and asked, "How long have you been doing it?"

It was starting to feel like an interrogation. "For a few years."

"What did you do before that?"

"I was a sales manager for a beauty company."

"Retired, huh?"

I choked on a laugh at the soft dig at my age. "I did take an early retirement."

She narrowed her shrewd gaze at me. "It must've been hard starting over. You know, at your age."

The digs were no longer soft. "I took a year off from my job to take care of my dying mother." Sorry, Mom, I thought. But I felt like she would approve, considering Rude Lorena looked like she'd just sucked a lemon. "After she passed away, I decided to stay in Garden Cove and start my business."

Lorena's arms dropped to her sides, and she shuffled her feet uncomfortably. "Sorry for your loss."

"Thanks. It's always hardest during the holidays." It was kind of mean to play the mom card, even if it wasn't a lie. I missed my mom something terrible, especially around Christmas, but Lorena had it coming.

The woman gaped at me then her eyes darted around the room as if looking for an exit. "Oh, everybody's getting food. Better go before the buffet's picked clean."

I gave her my most genuine smile. "Good idea."

Elaine came up to me after. "That was masterful."

I snorted. "I have no idea what you're talking about."

She laughed. "You lie, and I'll swear to it."

Ezra put drinks down on the table in front of two empty chairs. "You want to get dinner?"

"Yes." I took my coat off and put it on the back of a chair, and set my purse on the seat. I was still full from the pie and ice cream, but I'd passed some hot and sour soup on the buffet that looked like the perfect way to cap off a day of excellent food.

Ten minutes later, the long banquet table was a buzz with family, food, and chatter. I was spooning down the soup like it was going to run away from me if I didn't hurry while contemplating a second bowl. "This is so good," I said to Ezra.

"Mmm hmm," he agreed as he took a bite of General Tso's chicken.

"They're pretty consistent," Rose Marie, Lorena's daughter, informed me. "I like that in a restaurant." She had curly, dirty-blonde hair that framed her face like a lion's mane in the coolest way.

I nodded. "Me too."

"Sorry about my mom," she said. "She can be a little intense."

"She's fine." I gave a slight shrug. "Actually, I was expecting worse."

"Well, she's always been a little too protective. She's chased off more than one of my boyfriends over the years." She leaned a bit closer and spoke quietly when she said, "I haven't even told her about the new guy I'm dating."

"Yikes." I felt bad for Rose Marie, but on the other

hand, she was a grown woman who needed to learn how to set boundaries with her mother. "Is the relationship serious?"

"We've been going out for a couple of months," she confided.

Ezra put his hand on my leg and gave my thigh a squeeze. "You doing okay?" he asked.

"Yep." I slipped my hand over his. "No worries. I've been at business dinners with tougher crowds than your family."

"What is he doing here?" I heard someone hiss.

Ezra and I turned to look. Rob, Elaine's soon-to-be-ex, was standing in the doorway to the banquet room.

"Dad!" Prissy squealed. Tessa started crying, but that could've been because of the abrupt way her mother got up from her seat.

Elaine held up her hand when Hal and Lynn stood up. "I've got this," she said. "I can handle it."

The entire table had grown quiet except for Tessa's crying. Lynn came around the table and picked the little girl up from her booster, and started bouncing her.

Elaine stopped him before he reached the table. "Why are you here?"

He frowned and shook his head. "If any of you bothered to answer your phone, I wouldn't have had to show up unannounced."

"No one wants to talk to you," Lynn retorted. "This is a family-only dinner. You're not welcome."

"Mom," Elaine protested. "Let me handle this."

"Have any of you heard from Penny?" He looked around the table. "I was hoping she'd be here."

"You need to leave," Hal ordered, his voice hoarse and raspy.

I'm not sure what scent triggered the memory. It could've been all of them, but suddenly....

*"Mom. Dad. We're pregnant," a woman says. I recognize the voice as Elaine's. There was a man next to her and a couple across the booth table from them. "Rob and I wanted you both to know first."*

*"That's wonderful," the man across the table tells her. He has to be Hal, but his voice sounds more robust than it does now. "How far along are you?"*

*"Two months," Elaine says.*

*Lynn fidgets with her napkin. "My baby is having a baby. I'm so happy for you. I'm so pleased for the two of you."*

*"Thanks, Lynn," Rob says. "I can't wait to be her dad."*

*"Her?" Lynn pressed her fingers to her chest. "It's a girl."*

This is the restaurant where they announced their first child. I wasn't sure if the memory belonged to Rob, Elaine, Lynn, or Hal, but it had definitely been his arrival that triggered it.

"Why are you looking for Penny?" Lettie asked as I came out of the strong memory.

"Yeah, Rob," Hal accused. "Why are you looking for Penny?"

Rob's focus darted around the room, and he bit down on his lower lip for a second, then said, "Because I need to speak to her."

"There's nothing you need to say or do with Penny," Hal said. "She's your wife's cousin, for Heaven's sake."

"What's that supposed to mean?" Lettie asked.

"It means your trifling daughter has been trifling," Lynn intimated.

Elaine's face fell. "Is this true?" she asked Rob. "Are you seeing Penny?"

His eyes went wide, and he shook his head vehemently. "Of course not," he denied. "You know I wouldn't do that."

"I honestly don't know what you would or wouldn't do anymore," she said, then looked suddenly ashamed and embarrassed. Finally, she asked, "If you're not sleeping with her, then why do you want to find Penny?"

"Because she's in trouble." He scrubbed his bearded face with his palms, then took a calming breath. "She called me yesterday about an urgent matter."

"What matter?" Ezra asked.

"A good question," Rob replied. "One that I don't have the answers for. Penny was going to tell me at lunch today, but then you showed up at Weston's, and she clammed up. I was hoping someone here..." he scanned the faces at the table, "...might know something that could help me. Did any of you know why Penny wanted to talk to me?"

I could see the wheels spinning in Ezra's head. He glanced at Elaine and then back to Rob. "Why do you think she's in trouble now?"

He pulled out his phone and brought up a low-resolution video. "This is a security camera behind Trinity Bar and Grill at five-thirty tonight."

The whole family, except for the little ones, Ryan, and his girlfriend Amber, had gathered around.

"I have to warn you all. This might get a little too intense," Rob cautioned.

Lettie walked away and sat down. "Just tell me," she told Orsen. "I don't want to watch."

The low-quality recording on Rob's cell phone had today's date and a time stamp of *17:53:09*. It showed Penny waving her arm as if stretching as she stood on a step outside a door near a large trash bin. She was still wearing her red and green striped hat, the green tunic, and red tights.

A dark SUV, full-sized, drove past her. The way the camera pointed down from a high vantage point, it was impossible to see the driver or the license plate. When it stopped, only the side of the tail end was in view. The hatch on the back raised open. A few seconds later, someone in a full Santa suit with a beard and hat walked into the frame. He made a grab for Penny, and she jerked her arm back. She had a phone in her hand, and the Santa slapped her arm. The phone dropped to the ground, and he stomped on it. Penny then looked to be yelling as she wildly gesticulated at the man. It was hard to gauge height, but the Santa looked taller than her by a few inches.

"Is there volume?" Ezra asked.

Rob gave a quick head shake. "'Fraid not."

"Is that the guy she was fighting with at the parade?" I asked Ezra. "He seems a little different here, but it's hard to tell."

"Do you know who she was fighting with?" Rob hit the pause on the playback. "I mean, did you get his name?"

"Penny said she worked for him," I supplied. "If that's helpful."

"Clark Faber?" Lettie shook her head with disbelief. "Why would Penny fight with him? She liked her job, and she liked working for him."

Rob didn't comment. Instead, he tapped the play button and resumed the video.

Penny stepped back from the obviously yelling guy in the suit and fake beard. When she walked over to the opened hatch, another taller Santa came around the corner. He was holding something in his hand that, from this view, looked like it might be a weapon. Penny crawled into the back without a fight. Her face angled up, and I could see the anguish in her expression. My stomach churned as the hatch began to lower.

Rob turned off the video. "The video doesn't show what happened before or after. By the time the bar owner saw the video and checked the alleyway, the SUV was gone." He looked around at the family. "I'm afraid Penny's been taken."

# CHAPTER
# EIGHT

"That can't be Penny," Lettie insisted, though she still refused to look at the video. It was as if she thought if she didn't see it, then it couldn't have happened. "I don't believe it."

"This is preposterous," Orsen blustered. His balding head was beaded with sweat and beet red with worry. "Why would anyone...." His mouth twisted as his words trailed off.

"I'm going to call her right now. You'll see." Lettie took her phone from her purse and dialed her daughter. When Penny didn't answer, her lower lip began to tremble. "No," she denied. "I still don't believe it. She's just... busy."

Ezra and I took a step back as Orsen, Lynn, Hal, Lorena, Rollo, and Baxter circled Rob. For them, he was no longer the jerk who broke Elaine's heart. He was now a police officer doing his job and the only lifeline they had to their loved one's whereabouts.

Orsen's fear manifested as anger. "What are you doing to find my daughter?"

"Everything I can, including gathering as much information as possible to figure out what she had wanted to tell me this afternoon," Rob said with the same calmness I'd heard Ezra employ when talking to family members and witnesses during an investigation. He held up his phone, his screen frozen at the moment the second Santa came around the corner of the SUV. "Do any of you recognize either of these men? You all know Penny best. Is there anything familiar in the way the perpetrators move or walk? Anything that could give me a place to start looking?"

"It's hard to tell anything about them with them suits padded up and the beards," Rollo said. "They could be anybody."

"What about close friends?" Rob pressed. "Is there anyone she confides in?"

"There's Kathy Edwards," Baxter volunteered. "She and Penny have been best friends since high school."

Rob shook his head. "I tried Kathy. She says that she hasn't talked to Penny in a month."

"What about someone she's dating?" I asked, remembering the vision in the bathroom.

Lettie shook her head. "She was seeing someone earlier in the year, but I think they broke up. She never would tell me who it was." Her face pinched. "I think he might've been married." I could see it cost Lettie a lot to admit her daughter might have been a mistress, and I admired her willingness to be truthful in the current situation.

Ezra inserted himself into the mix. "Who reported the recording?"

"The owner of Trinity bar, Ralph Conroy. He's got a motion sensor camera set up to record events in the alley near his delivery door when it detects humans, not vehicles. A few seconds after they are out of frame, the recording stops." Rob popped his jaw and rubbed his chin. "Unfortunately, the camera has no playback capability to see what happened before or after."

"Why was she in the alley behind Trinity bar?" Rollo asked.

"We found her car in a parking space in front of the bar," Rob said. "We've towed it to the impound lot for safe keeping."

I snapped up my hand. "What about the guy she was arguing with at the restaurant this afternoon. Could he be one of the Santas?" It felt weird to keep calling the assailants Santas, but it was the most expedient way to identify them. "He was angry enough to push her around in a parking lot full of witnesses."

"When was this?" Rob asked.

"After you left," Ezra said. "I chased the guy off. He ran across the road to the gas station. Penny wouldn't say who it was. She just told me to mind my own business."

Rob glared at Ezra. "And you're just telling me now?"

"Yes," he answered. "How could I have known to tell you sooner?"

I thought the more immediate suspect was the guy she was fighting with at the parade. Was he the same person who'd confronted her in the parking lot? I regarded Rob for a moment. "Have you talked to her boss yet?"

He waved off my question. "When you get a badge, then you can ask the questions."

"I have a badge," Ezra said.

"But you have no jurisdiction."

"Robert Allen Phillips, you watch yourself," Lynn hissed as she continued to bounce Tessa on her hip. "My niece is missing, and by your own words, she's in danger, and you're going to come in here and sass my son? A seasoned detective who specializes in this kind of investigation? Is that how you're going to behave after we've opened our homes and our hearts to you over the past seven years? Your betrayal knows no bounds, apparently."

Rob managed to shrink under Lynn's admonishment. He couldn't meet her harsh stare. Frankly, I thought she was glorious. I had a lot of respect for law enforcement. Some of the most important people in my life were or had been on the job. However, Rob deserved that dressing down. He was wasting time and being a general putz.

"Sorry," he apologized. "I'm trying to do my job."

Lynn handed her quieted two-year-old grand-daughter off to Lorena. "Do it better."

"We can come down to the station tonight and give a statement about what we saw at Weston's," Ezra told him. "Nora talked to Penny briefly at the restaurant, but she didn't say much."

"Other than a whole lot of mind your own business," I admitted.

"That's not necessary." Rob's hands were shaking. "I'll let you know if we need to take more formal statements."

It didn't take being a psychic to know that something was off. Rob was withholding information. That was expected in an active investigation. However, whatever he was keeping from the family had him feeling anxious.

Lettie started to cry. Her sisters were instantly at her side, offering soothing comforts. Baxter had gotten on his phone and started making calls. The other brother, Rollo, said, "That's it. I'm not going to sit around here all night while Deputy Dumbass gets my sister killed. I'm going to look for her."

Rob jammed his hands in his coat pockets. "Rollo, if you have any idea where I should start looking, I'd love to know."

"Everyone needs to calm down," Ezra suggested. I could see him mentally compartmentalizing as he prioritized the work over his personal feelings about his brother-in-law. "Rob is trying to do his job. I'm sure there are several police officers out canvasing the town and surrounding areas for any signs of Penny."

"Yes," Rob said. "We have officers actively searching for her and the culprits." He nodded his thanks to Ezra, then took his hand out of his pocket and pointed at the door to the banquet room. "Can I talk to you privately for a moment?"

"Oh, thank heavens," Elaine said with exasperation.

Rob thinned his lips but barely looked at her.

Ezra's glance at me was questioning. It was his way of asking if I wanted to be involved.

I nodded in the affirmative. If there was a chance my psychic sense could help find Penny before something tragic happened to her, I had to try.

Ezra returned his attention to his brother-in-law. "Sure. Nora's coming with me."

"Why?" Rob asked. "Is she a detective too?"

"Of a sort," Ezra explained. "She's a consultant for the Garden Cove PD. She has a special set of skills that could be useful."

"Like Liam Neeson," Rose Marie's son Ryan chimed in. He earned several angry stares with the comment, especially from Lorena, his grandmother. The young man shrugged. "Sorry."

Lorena waggled a finger at me. "I thought you make soaps." She made it sound like an indictment.

Elaine stepped in to shut the older woman up. "If Ezra thinks Nora should be involved, then she should be involved, and you should stay out of it."

Lorena managed to look offended, but she didn't protest again.

Rob sized me up for a moment before telling Ezra, "Fine. I'll meet you both out front."

I arched a brow at Ezra, and he shrugged. "Are you sure you're okay with this?"

"She's your cousin," I told him. "If I can help, I want to."

Elaine came over to us. "Do you think Penny's going to be all right?"

"It depends on a lot of factors," Ezra replied. "The first twenty-four hours are the most important. We'll assist Rob as much as he'll let us."

"And if he doesn't let us," I added, "We'll investigate on our own."

"What she said." Ezra regarded me with a warm and tender expression that melted me to the core.

His sister angled close and said in a quiet voice, "Thank you for offering to help. We're grateful for anything you, uh, manage to, uhm, woo-woo out."

Huh. Was Elaine aware of my gift? Had Ezra told her? If he had, I wasn't sure how I felt about it. On one hand, I was glad he felt like he could confide in his sister. On the other hand, it hit me weird that she knew, and I hadn't been aware of it.

"I'll do what I can," I said.

Elaine looked over her shoulder at her aunts, parents, uncle, and cousins and said to Ezra, "You'll let us know if you all find out anything."

He inclined his head. "As long as it doesn't interfere with locating Penny, I'll make sure you're kept in the loop."

Elaine nudged him with her elbow. "Go find out what the jerk has to say. Call me later."

I walked away from Ezra and went to get our coats from the chairs. My purse was on the floor. It was unzipped, so when I picked it up, my coin purse fell out. I tucked it back in and zipped it up.

Lorena grasped my elbow, her claw-like fingers pinching. "How can you possibly help? You should stay out of it. You'll just get in the way."

I gently extricated myself from the woman who was obviously spoiling for a fight. I gave her a thin smile. "I know you're upset, but I've helped the police with several investigations, and if I can do anything in my power to find your niece, then I have to try."

She raised both brows at me. "I don't buy your nicey-nice act," she snarled. "And I swear, if this—"

"That's enough," Lynn confronted her sister. "We all have enough to worry about without you stirring up trouble."

"I'm just—"

Lynn snorted. "I know exactly what you're doing, and I want you to stop."

"Everything okay?" Ezra asked as he came over and took his jacket from me.

"It's all fine," I replied, feeling out of sorts. I put on

my jacket and slung my purse over my shoulder. "Let's go see a man about a missing girl."

---

I DANCED on my toes as we exited the restaurant to try and stave off the chilly temperature. "You told Elaine about my ability." It was a statement, not a question.

"I didn't tell her exactly about your gifts. Elaine follows my cases, and there was a Stupor post about a case that you helped solve."

Stupor was the true crime equivalent of TMZ. It was a sensationalized news website that based its stories on facts but dramatized the cases for clicks. "Which case?"

"Aaron Trident," Ezra answered. "You know how high profile that investigation was. Something was bound to get out."

Considering Trident had been our town mayor, the case had briefly made national news. But my part in the case had been kept out of the headlines. "How did Stupor get the story?"

"Trident's lawyer leaked a letter from him, where he accused the Garden Cove PD of employing an unnamed psychic, and that the evidence against him was tainted, and his case should be thrown out."

"Ridiculous," I sneered. "The man murdered his lover, then kidnapped Pippa and was going to kill her."

"He still won't take a plea. His lawyer got him another postponement last month," Ezra said.

The law moved slowly. It was no surprise that the trial had been postponed. Some cases took years to prosecute. Because of the first-degree murder charge, Trident had been denied bail. The only saving grace in the whole process. "So, Elaine asked who the psychic was, huh?"

"She specifically asked me if it was you. I think she had her suspicions based on a few of our conversations about other cases you helped me with when I told her about how we met." He gave me a look that radiated affection. "That said, I didn't give her any details about your ability. I just didn't deny it when she asked. We've only recently started to reconnect, and I didn't want to outright lie."

"I get that." I gently nudged him with my elbow. "I wish you would've told me, though, that she knew."

"I should've said something," he acknowledged. "I'm sorry. I respect your gift, Nora, but more than that, I respect how capable you are under pressure. Even without your aroma mojo, you would be a damn fine detective."

"Thanks," I told him. It was hard to be upset when he said things like that. "Apology accepted," I said on a *brrrrr*. I dug my mittens from my pockets. "Why couldn't we meet inside? You know, where the heaters work." I realized complaining about the cold weather was petty compared to whatever Penny was going through right now. "You must be worried about your cousin, and here I am going on about what Elaine does or doesn't know."

"I'm concerned," he agreed. "Penny and I aren't close, but I want her back home safe."

I had a few cousins that I barely knew. If something happened to them, I'd feel bad in the way I'd feel bad if anything happened to any friendly acquaintance. It wouldn't devastate me, though. Not the way it hurts to lose a loved one. Still, like Ezra, I wanted to do everything I could to get Penny back to her family.

I saw Rob standing by a dark truck. It was hard to tell, even with the streetlamps, the exact color. He waved at us.

We crossed the short distance to him. His vehicle was running.

"Get in the truck," Rob said. "I've got the heater on."

It was a double cab, and I climbed in the back. Ezra got in on the passenger side.

There was a cardboard box in the backseat. While the overhead light was on, I opened the flap and saw a notebook and a clear plastic baggie with a cell phone inside it. The screen was cracked. Was that Penny's from the video? Most likely. I wondered why it was in Rob's truck and not at the police station being cataloged as evidence. The light went out before I could see more.

"What do you want to tell me?" Ezra asked when we were settled in with the doors closed.

Rob paused for a moment, probably trying to decide how much information he should give up. His frown deepened as he turned to Ezra. "Penny called me yesterday and said she was in trouble and that it involved the Santa Walk. I wasn't sure how serious to take her claim, but this afternoon she told me that she was in danger and that she was scared."

Ezra's face went stony. "Did she say who she was afraid of?"

"She didn't say who, but something did happen after the parade tonight. Something other than Penny going missing."

"What do you mean? I asked. "What happened?"

Rob stretched his neck, and it cracked. "The charity money from the Santa Walk has been stolen."

"Holy crap." I leaned forward. "How much was taken?"

"Twenty thousand dollars. The most money ever raised for this event minus Pike matching the funds."

"Ho boy." I said, "Talk about a bombshell."

CHAPTER

# NINE

E zra got eerily calm. "Do you have any leads at all?"
"I've got a little over a hundred suspects," Rob
said. "Unfortunately, it's hard to tell the regular Santas
apart from the criminal ones, and we don't have the
manpower to check every one of their alibis."

"How does someone walk off with that much charity
money without anyone noticing?" I asked.

"This was organized down to the letter," Rob said
evasively as he tapped his thumb against the steering
wheel. "I think Penny might have been involved in some
way. After all, she helped organize the event and had
inside information about how and when the money
would be handed off and transferred to the bank."

"That's a load of horse crap," Ezra told him. "Why
would she call you if she was in on it?"

"Remorse," Rob said defensively. "I mean, who
knows? I'm not going to interpret the evidence to fit

what I think might've happened. I have to go where it leads. You know that as well as I do."

Ezra shook his head. "So, are you treating her disappearance as if she's on the run or that she's been abducted?"

"The official line is that she's been taken against her will, but the chief wants this handled quickly, and he wants Penny arrested if it turns out she's involved. He's worried about how losing this much charity money reflects on the Hillside Police Department. We had a lot of officers out today, and all this went down without anyone catching a whiff of it."

"Where was the money being kept?" I asked. "And weren't people looking after it?"

"I'd like to know as well," Ezra agreed.

"Clark Faber had the money in a portable fire-safe in the trunk of his car."

"Which brings me back to my earlier question," Ezra said. "Have you talked to Faber?"

Rob let out a slow breath. "We found Faber in a field outside of town by his blue Cadillac CRS with the trunk open and his head kicked in."

"Dead?" I asked, surprised by this revelation.

"No," Rob answered. "But he hasn't regained consciousness yet, so we can't ask him what happened."

"Was he driven out to the field? Or did he drive himself?" Ezra asked.

Rob spread his fingers. "That's the question, isn't it?"

I tapped Ezra's shoulder. "Wasn't he military?" Hal

had said Faber retired at twenty years. "A career man would know how to defend himself, right? Was there any sign that the person who assaulted him might be injured as well?"

"There was blood at the scene. It would be next to impossible to determine if any of it is someone else's."

I knew that real investigations weren't like police television shows. Evidence took days, weeks, and sometimes months to process. And most of the time, unless there was a strong reason, it was too expensive for the police departments to run tests on every part of a crime scene. It usually came down to fingerprints, blood, and physical evidence. If there was a lot of blood, it would be hard for the forensic team to discern a few drops of foreign blood.

"How do you know the safe was in the trunk?" Ezra inquired. "If it was gone when you found him, maybe it was never there."

"The safe was still in the trunk," Rob said. "Whoever stole the money had to have had the combination because the safe was wide open." He held up a hand. "And before you ask, the plant manager confirmed that Faber was taking care of the money, and the two women working the collections saw him put the safe they handed off to him in the trunk. The plan was for him to put it in a bigger, more secure safe at Pike Manufacturing until they could deposit it into the bank after Christmas."

There was something about this caper that didn't

make much sense to me. "I know twenty thousand dollars is a lot, but is it enough to warrant an elaborate heist?"

"I was thinking the same thing." Rob flipped the air vent folds away from him. "It makes no sense. I mean, if there are two people involved, that's ten K each. And if Penny was involved, and it was split three ways, even less money."

"I've seen criminals do more for less," Ezra commented. "For some people, that much money looks like a fortune."

"What about the assault? He got handily thrashed. You don't kick someone's head in unless it's personal. Maybe the motive isn't strictly greed, but revenge." The heat from the vent blasted my face, and I moved from its path. I was still a little cold, but the hot air was drying out my eyes. "Maybe disgruntled employees?"

Rob considered my suggestion, then nodded. "Possible. Faber is human resources. I'm sure he's had to let go of his fair share of employees for cause. I'll call the plant manager to get a list of recent fires."

I shrugged. "Or maybe they thought it would be more money."

"Again, possible."

"How did you find Faber so quickly?" Ezra asked.

"A farmer was checking on his cows' water troughs to make sure they weren't frozen. He saw the car, went and checked, then found Faber. Luckily, everyone has cellphones these days, and he called nine-one-one.

Faber's injuries were bad enough that if he hadn't been found so quickly, he probably wouldn't have survived."

"I guess that's something."

"Can you hand me that box?" Rob asked me.

"Sure." I slid it onto my lap and lifted it into the front.

Rob took it from me and rummaged to the bottom. "Here," he said. "I found this in Faber's wallet."

Ezra's expression was as surprised as mine. It was a photo of Penny dressed like Princess Leia from Star Wars, and there was a slightly taller Chewbacca with his arms wrapped around her from behind. On the back of the photo, there was a note that said, *I'm so glad I kissed a Wookie. xoxo, P.*

"That's weird, right?" Ezra asked. "And not just the note. Do you think that's Faber under all that fur?"

"Hard to tell." Rob shrugged. "But it was in the man's possessions, so chances are good."

"They were probably at a science fiction convention," I mused. "I grew up with Star Wars, and there was a time in my life that I might've been tempted to dress up as Leia." I stared at the photo. "Only, I would have picked her rebellion outfit from *A New Hope* and not the harem bikini from *Return of the Jedi.*"

"Nerd." Ezra smiled at me. "Every time I think I know all there is to know about you...."

"I have many layers," I told him.

"Looking forward to peeling them all back." He lowered his brows at Rob. "So, how does Penny play into this. If she was in a relationship with Faber, then why would she also be working with the thieves?"

"Your guess is as good as mine." Rob reached out and gripped the steering wheel, his knuckles going white. "I wish I'd tried harder this afternoon. I wish I knew what she'd wanted to tell me. I could've prevented all of this."

"Hindsight makes everyone an expert." Ezra shook his head. "You can't look back. That's not going to help us find Penny."

I'd found out that my smell-o-vision worked best with strong emotions. Penny had been taken near a garbage bin. If it had a strong odor, there was a chance the memory of the abduction might be attached. "I think we should check out the alley behind the bar."

Rob's gaze met mine. "Ezra said you were a consultant. What's your specialty?"

I glanced at Ezra, unsure how much I should divulge. He nodded for me to go ahead and tell the truth.

"I get psychic visions," I stated.

"Oh, for the love of Pete," Rob sputtered. He fixed his stare at Ezra. "Tell me you're not serious. You don't believe in all that nonsense, do you?"

I winced at Rob's reaction but calmly said, "You and Elaine told Hal and Lynn you were pregnant with Prissy in a booth at the Oriental Palace Buffet. You guys wanted them to be the first to know."

He squinted at me. "Elaine or her parents could've told you that story."

"But they didn't," I assured him. "You were wearing

a green t-shirt, and Elaine was in a pale blue summer dress. You'd found out it was a girl, and you were excited to be her dad."

Rob's frown deepened. "What else have you seen about me?"

"Nothing," I admitted. "I got that vision when you first walked into the banquet room tonight. I imagine it was the scent of the food that reminded you of that night."

"I don't remember what I wore." His focus grew distant as he absently gave his beard a stroke. "But I remember Elaine's dress." Whatever had happened between them, Rob still loved Elaine. "Telling Hal and Lynn had made it real."

"Made what real?" Ezra asked.

"Our family. Before that moment, it had just been the two of us, and sharing the news made us more than that."

"That makes sense." I shifted in my seat to give my knees more room. "I get visions when a scent is tied to an important memory. The more emotional the memory, the stronger the vision."

Rob's head quirked to one side as he stared at me for a moment as if trying to make up his mind. In the end, he nodded his affirmation. "I'm willing to suspend my disbelief.... For now."

"Good," Ezra told him. "Now, let's stop wasting time Penny might not have and take Nora to the alley."

CHAPTER

# TEN

On the way over, Rob went through what he knew about the victim. Clark Faber was a thirty-nine-year-old, single, white male with no children. He had no arrests on record, apart from a speeding ticket in 2012 in San Antonio, Texas. He'd put in a request for military records, but it was the week of Christmas, so there was little hope of getting any information from the air force before the new year.

Rob parked near the alley behind Trinity Bar and Grill. The bar itself was closed for the holiday and wouldn't be opening back up again until the twenty-seventh. The area between buildings was wide enough for delivery trucks to get through, and the poorly maintained asphalt had large cracks created by cold days meeting hot days and vice versa. Typical of Missouri.

I pulled the hood up on my coat and pulled the cinch string to keep the wind from stinging my ears. I worried that the cold would dampen any lingering odors in the area. Much like a refrigerator, winter had a way of keeping garbage from spoiling.

The whirring sound of a heat pump fan and the hum of a flickering sodium streetlamp gave the area a spooky feel. The yellow light from the lamp added to the eerie quality. Rob led us to the bar's back door, then pointed up at the camera mounted about ten feet up on the building across the street.

"Does the owner of the bar own that building as well?" Ezra asked.

"No," Rob said. "That's Mega-shield Insurance. It's owned by Darcy Adams, but according to Conroy, Ms. Adams gave him permission to mount the camera there, as long as he shared anything that might be relevant to her business."

I crossed my arms over my chest as an idea struck me as more than coincidental. "How long has the camera been up?"

Rob came around the left side of me and put his foot on the concrete step at the base of the door. "Do you think it's important?"

"Maybe."

He gave me a skeptical look but pulled out his phone and hit a number already on his call list. He put it on speaker and held it out between us. After a few seconds, a man answered. "Hello?"

"Mr. Conroy, this is Detective Phillips from the Hillside PD. We spoke earlier."

"Yes, Detective. What can I do for you?"

Rob cleared his throat. "How long has your security camera been up in the alley?"

"For four years," Conroy replied. "I put it up after my bar was broken into."

"And, just to clarify, your neighbor Ms. Adams is aware the camera is mounted on her building?"

"Yes, sir. She is fully aware."

"Thank you for your time," Rob said. After he hung up, he stared at me. "Well? Did that call tell you anything?" He gestured meaningfully at his head with a twirling finger.

I frowned. "If you mean did I have a vision, then no. That's not how it works for me."

"Then why did you want to know how long the camera has been up?"

"Something Lynn said this afternoon when she and Hal were talking about Penny working at Pike Manufacturing."

"Oh, right," Ezra said with a nod. "Penny worked at Mega-Shield Insurance. I'd forgotten about that."

"Exactly," I enthused, quite pleased I'd remembered. "And, if the camera has been up for a while, and Ms. Adams was aware, chances are good, Penny, as her employee, might've known about the camera too."

Rob sucked in a breath, then coughed as the cold air hit the back of his throat. When he could, he said, "If you're right, then Penny knew she was being recorded."

Ezra cast a sweeping glance around the empty alley.

"Which means she might have left some kind of crumb for us to follow."

Rob chewed the inside of his cheek for a moment, then shook his head. "We searched the area after Conroy reported the video. We didn't find anything other than her broken phone."

"We should look at that video again," I said. "You might've missed something, or some signal from Penny, without realizing."

Rob took his phone from his pocket. Big, wet flakes of snow hit the glass and melted into fat drops. "Crap," Rob said. "This snow is going to make the situation even more difficult."

"Then we need to hurry before the trail goes cold," I said. Both men stared at me as if I'd grown an extra nostril. I gave them a wry look. "You know what I mean."

Without any fanfare, Rob opened the gallery on his phone and tapped the video folder.

"It'd be nice if there was sound," Ezra mused.

"Would've made this a whole lot easier," Rob agreed.

The snow doubled in volume, and I blinked as flakes hit my eyelashes. "We should hurry this along."

"Here," Rob said. We huddled over the screen to keep it from getting wet. "This is where she triggers the motion sensor."

We watched Penny's arm raise over her head twice at the beginning of the clip. It made me wonder if she'd done it a few times before the recording had started trying to trigger the camera into action.

"The Santa guy arrived right behind her." I indicated the moving vehicle. "Do you think she had planned to meet him there? In the alley, I mean? It can't be a coincidence, right?"

Ezra pointed at the screen. "What's she doing there?"

While Penny gesticulated her anger with one hand, she waved the other at her hip. "I see it," I said. "Did she throw something?"

"Her hand moved in the direction of that drainpipe." Rob waved his hand at a six-inch diameter pipe strapped to the side of the building.

I handed Ezra a small pink flashlight I had in my purse. It had been a stocking stuffer gift from him the previous year. He gave me a crooked smile as he clicked it on and crouched next to the pipe to investigate its base and the surrounding area.

I took the opportunity to go smell garbage. Ick. I was correct about the cold weather dampening the stench.

"Anything," Rob asked.

"Nothing," we both said at the same time before we locked gazes.

"Jinx," I said. "You owe me a Diet Coke."

"Done." Ezra stood up, and the flashlight beam caused something shiny on the ground to glint.

"What's that?" I walked over to where I'd seen it, a

few feet from the drain. "Shine that light back over here."

Rob made his way over as Ezra swung the flashlight in my direction. I saw the glimmer of metal again. "Aha!" I dug a clean tissue from my purse and picked up the item. "It's a key."

"A key to what?"

I held it out to him. "It looks like my house key, but who knows."

Rob took it. "The grooves have rough tool marks. I think this might be a duplicate of the original key."

"What do you think it fits?"

"A house, a lockbox, a locker.... There are too many options," Rob said.

Ezra brought the light closer. "Agreed. There are too many options."

"Apartment," Rob said. "She lives in a one-bedroom apartment over on Grand Avenue."

"If Penny threw it away to prevent her abductors from taking it, then it must be to something important. We should go see if this key fits anything there." It would also give me the opportunity to investigate any lingering aromas.

Rob shook his head. "I'll need to get a warrant."

"How long will that take?" I asked. "What if Penny doesn't have that much time?"

"Whether Penny's involved or not, it's illegal to search someone's home without probable cause, and her being missing isn't enough to go break into her place,"

Ezra said, agreeing with Rob. "However, a concerned family member with a key could go in and look around. And if he or she found something of importance, they could notify the police...." He let the implication lie.

"That's walking a thin line," Rob said.

Ezra nodded. "Really thin, but not illegal."

Rob didn't look happy about it, but he said, "Okay. Let's do it. Where are we going to get a key?"

Ezra retrieved his phone. Hesitantly, he said, "I'll call mom and see if Aunt Lettie has a spare."

CHAPTER

# ELEVEN

S now started to pile up as Ezra, Rob, and I waited in the comfort of Rob's truck at the Grand Apartments on Grand Avenue. Fortunately, Lettie had been in possession of a spare key, but she'd had to go home to retrieve it. Fifteen minutes later, Lynn, Lettie, and, unfortunately, Lorena arrived in a small four-door sedan. The sisters piled out of the vehicle, looking like they were geared up for an Arctic exploration.

Donning oversized coats with the hoods pulled up, thick gloves, and quilted snow boots, the sisters met us in the parking lot, and as a group, we went into the apartment complex and up the stairs to the second floor.

"These knees are not made for stairs," Lorena complained. "They need an elevator in this place."

"You didn't have to come," Lettie snapped back, sounding like she'd had about all she could take of her oldest sister. "As a matter of fact, you weren't invited."

"Would you two stop it," Lynn said. "Sniping at each other is just going to make a bad situation worse."

Ezra, Rob, and I were smart enough to keep our opinions to ourselves. When we got to apartment 22b, Lettie handed Ezra the keys. "Can I go in with you?" she asked.

"It's better if you stay out here for the moment. I don't know what we'll find," he said, his voice filled with compassion. "You guys can keep Rob company while Nora and I take a quick look around."

"Land sakes," Lorena griped. "Your cougar is allowed to traipse around in the heated apartment while we have to stand out here in the cold. Why am I not surprised?"

My mouth dropped open as if someone had loosened the bolts on a hinge.

Lynn's shock was apparent as her gaze darted back and forth between Ezra, Lorena, and me.

"Aunt Lorena." Ezra's tone held a warning. "Don't talk about Nora like that."

"Well, I don't know what the kids are calling a woman like her these days? A sugar mama? Cradle snatcher? Milk?"

"Milf," Lettie corrected absently.

Lynn shot her younger sister a look. "Don't help her."

Lettie grimaced. "Sorry."

Ezra's face was getting red, and it wasn't from the cold.

Rob, smartly, had taken two steps back. I imagined he was grateful the negative attention was on someone other than himself.

Lorena gave me a curt nod. "That's it, MILF. A mother Ezra would like to—"

Before she could finish, I hawed a laugh, the sound akin to a donkey's bray, and I kept laughing. I hadn't been sure how I'd react if his family had a problem with our age difference, but now I knew. I'd expected some backhanded remarks and quiet digs, but Lorena was completely in-my-face absurd. I was appalled but also a little impressed.

Lynn and Lettie rapidly shifted their gaze from me to their rude sister. The rude sister looked like she was going to swallow her tongue. The woman had wanted a smackdown, but instead, she was the star of her own comedy show.

Ezra wore an unhappy frown, but I saw Rob smirk as Lorena's mouth opened, closed, opened, and closed again.

"What's so funny?" the Bitter Betty finally asked.

I took a couple deep breaths, and my humor faded. "I'm not a mother," I said flatly. I turned my attention to Ezra. "Let's get in there before everyone gets frostbite." I resisted the urge to add a "meow" at the end of the statement. Point for me.

I could hear the sisters whispering fiercely as Ezra and I went into the apartment.

Ezra dipped his shoulder to mine. "You shut her the hell up. That's a first."

"That woman has got a big ol' bug up her behind about me." I'd thought Ezra's mom would be the tough sell, but she'd been a real peach. Lorena, however, was doing her damnedest to run me off. "What's that all about?"

"There are some people, like my Aunt Lettie, that don't have a mean bone in their body, and that's because my Aunt Lorena got them all."

I snorted. "Funny."

"Accurate," he said. "But now that I know that laughter is literally the cure for Lorena-itis, I'll be employing the Nora-method whenever she tries to start some crap with me."

We studied the apartment. It was a basic box with a living room and kitchen taking up the front half when you entered, and there was an opening recessed into the wall near the end of the kitchen cabinets that had three doors. The two facing each other were most likely the bathroom and bedroom and the smaller door, the linen closet.

Penny had made a minimal effort to decorate with a small pre-lit green Christmas tree sitting on top of an electric heater in the living room. The furniture consisted of a taupe vinyl couch, matching chair and ottoman. The vinyl had flaked in places, and there was a dark stain on the arm of the couch. Oddly, even with the furniture and the tree, the place felt cold and empty.

"Where do you want to start?" he asked.

Kitchens and living rooms tended to have more PG-rated memories, while bedrooms and bathrooms were likely NSFN. Not safe for Nora. Still, they were usually the places where the strongest memories went down.

However, I recognized the fridge with the dent and deep scratch. This is where Penny's kitchen memory had been located. "I'll start in here and work my way to the other rooms."

Ezra opened the door on the left. "Bathroom," he said. Then he opened the one on the right. "Bedroom." He went into that room first.

I began by checking the cabinets, popping the tops off canisters situated on the counter, and opening the fridge. There was one thing clearly evident, Penny hadn't stocked any new items in a while, and almost everything was empty. There was a jar of peanut butter in the cupboard, a loaf of bread in a drawer, and a half dozen eggs, a quart of milk, and some butter in the fridge. Nothing else. Even the coffee canister was down to a few scoops of grounds at the bottom.

I picked the canister up and brought it to my nose....

*"God, I love the scent of fresh Columbian," a thin woman with dark blonde hair styled down around her shoulders says. "It's the true champion of coffee drinkers."*

*A man with brown hair sits on the couch. He positions himself sideways to face the woman in the kitchen. "As long as it's hot and black, I'll drink it."*

*"The military ruined you for good coffee," she says with a laugh. "But one steaming cup, coming right up."*

*He chuckles and teases, "I could fall in love with a woman like you."*

*Her tone turns serious. "A woman like me could fall in love with you."*

As the memory fades, I can still feel the tenderness of the moment. The military comment gave more credence to the idea that there was a personal relationship between Penny and Clark Faber. It still didn't answer the question about why they were fighting today. Had he found out about the plot to steal the charity money? Had the fight been a confrontation? I still didn't understand how he ended up in a farm field outside of town. Whatever the reason, I wasn't going to find out in the kitchen.

There were no scented candles, room sprays, or lotions in the living room. The Christmas tree was unscented as well. I'm sure it was strange seeing me sniff my way through the kitchen and living room, but the sisters had managed to keep their voices low enough that I couldn't hear what they were saying.

Until I started sniffing the couch.

"What is she?" Lorena asked. "The fart detective? A butt hound?"

"Shut up," Lynn hissed.

"Cracking cases, one derriere at a time," Lorena continued.

I nearly choked on my own spit at her comment. Luckily, I managed to keep it together. When I got to the arm with the stain, I caught a redolent chemical tang. It smelled a bit like cleaning chemicals with a slight lemon undertone.

*"You're bleeding." The dark blonde woman, Penny, I assume, ushers a man inside the apartment. The guy is taller than the woman, and his brown hair reminds me of the man from the previous vision, but it's cut differently, and it's messy as if he's been in a tussle. "Sit down," she tells him. "I'll get some paper towels."*

*She rushes into the kitchen and grabs a roll from the counter. Blood is dripping down the guy's hand onto the arm of the couch. She rips a wad of sheets from the roll and hands it to him to stem the flow.*

*"Thank you," he says, pressing the paper towels against his forearm. "I didn't know where else to go."*

*"What happened?" she asks.*

*"I can't...." His voice is shaky and rough. I can't tell if it's the same man as her coffee date. He doesn't sound the same, but he's upset, and that can change a tone of voice. "I don't want to talk about it," he says. "I just need a minute."*

*"Let me see it." She turns his arm over. A jagged laceration on his forearm oozes red. "That's deep. It's going to need stitches," she says. "You need to go to the emergency room."*

*"No." He jerks his arm back protectively, then presses the towels onto his wound again. "I'll be fine. I've had worse. No hospital."*

I let out a harsh breath when the vision ended. My palm was pressed against the stain. I recoiled from the spot. Ezra came out of the bedroom.

"Anything?" he asked.

"Nothing helpful," I told him. "You?"

"Something," he replied. "Penny's bedroom is empty."

"What do you mean?" Lettie hollered from the door. "How is it empty?"

He scratched his nose and gestured toward the bedroom. "Her clothes, her personal stuff, everything, is gone. Even the bed sheets have been stripped." Ezra's lips thinned. "Penny packed up to leave town."

"You can't know that," Lorena scoffed.

"I'm afraid it's true." That's when I noticed he had an envelope in his hand. "She left a goodbye note."

# TWELVE

Lorena brusquely shoved past her sisters. "Let me see the letter."

Ezra's arm went back and up as if he were playing a game of keep-away from his aunt.

"Calm down, Lorena." Lynn grabbed her sister's wrist. "This is Lettie's to handle."

A noise of disagreement escaped the eldest of the sisters. "That would be a first."

Lettie, who trailed inside behind them, wore a forlorn expression that made me sorry for her. It had to be difficult finding out that your child was running away and the only goodbye was in the form of a letter.

"Is it handwritten?" Lorena asked. "Because if it's typed, it could be a fake. I've watched enough Agatha Christie movies to know that you never trust a typed letter."

"It's handwritten," Ezra said, throwing her a bone.

Hopefully, not another mean one. "Aunt Lettie, do you want to read it?"

Lettie took her gloves off and set them on the kitchen counter. Her hand trembled as she nodded to Ezra and reached for the letter.

Rob closed the door to the apartment, and the living room instantly felt warmer. "That's evidence," he said.

"No, it isn't," Ezra told him. "Not yet. As far as the police are concerned, this letter doesn't exist until after Aunt Lettie reads it. It's addressed to her and Uncle Orsen."

Rob paused for a moment, then acquiesced. "Fine, but once Lettie's done, I'm taking it for processing."

Ezra agreed. "Deal." He gave the letter to Lettie. She walked over to the counter and took it out of the envelope. She made several heartbreaking sounds as she read through it. "Oh, Penny," she sighed. "What have you done?"

Lynn strolled over to her sister and put her arm around her. "What's it say?"

"She says she's finally got enough money to get Kyle, and she's going to get him, and they are going to give him the family he deserves. She doesn't want me to look for her." Lettie's eyes watered with unshed tears. "She's happy for the first time in a long time, and...." A barking sob erupted from the youngest sister's throat. She put her hand to her mouth. "She loves me, but she wants me to let her go."

Yikes. The letter sounded a little damning. Charity

money gets stolen, and Penny writes a letter saying she finally has enough money to get her son and start over? It wasn't a direct admission of guilt, but it could be interpreted that way.

"I'm sorry, Lettie, but I'm going to need that letter now," Rob held out his hand palm up and did the gimme curl. "There's enough in there for probable cause for a warrant."

Lorena, who had moved to the other side of Lettie, snatched the letter from her sister's hand. Lettie cried out in dismay, and she gasped when Lorena took a lighter from her pocket and lit the letter on fire.

"What are you doing?" Rob exclaimed. He rushed forward, but Lorena was faster than he calculated, and she was around the counter and at the sink before he could reach her.

Lorena held out her free hand to fend off Rob. "Get back," she demanded as she dropped the burning confession into the sink, turned on the water, shoved the wet paper into the garbage disposal and flipped the switch.

I was so flabbergasted. All I could do was stand there and watch the drama play out. Ezra didn't make a move to stop her, either.

There were a lot of angry words exchanged as Rob got past Lorena's slapping hand and jostled the older woman away from the sink with his hip. He turned the disposal off, but it was too late. The letter was gone.

"Why in the world would you do that? You destroyed evidence in an active case. I could arrest you."

Lorena scowled at him. "I don't know what you're talking about, Officer Phillips. I haven't seen any letter that could be used as evidence against my abducted niece." She turned her glower at the rest of us. "Have any of you seen such a letter?"

Lettie, who initially looked as if she would protest, gave her sister a grateful nod. "I haven't seen any letter," she said.

Lynn piped up. "Me either." She glanced at her son. "Ezra, have you seen a letter that could potentially implicate your cousin in her own disappearance?"

He shook his head. "I don't see any letter." I noticed the tense shift to the present. He didn't want to lie, but he also wanted to back his family.

Lynn asked me next. "What about you, Nora?"

"I can say with one hundred percent honesty that I have not seen the letter." Technically, I'd only seen the envelope, and I had not been shown the contents.

I gave Lorena an assessing look. Trashing the letter before Rob could get a hold of it had been a calculated play to protect her sister. The old bitch was a smart cookie.

"I give up." Rob swatted at the air as if he could wave away the stench of cover-up. "Thank you, ladies, for bringing the key to the apartment. You may go now before any other evidence ends up in the garbage disposal."

Lorena walked Lettie out. Lynn glanced back at me. "See you and Ezra tomorrow?"

"Yes," I told her. "We'll call you in the morning."

She nodded to her son. "See you soon."

"Bye, Mom," he said. "Try not to worry. I'm going to do everything I can to find Penny."

"Me too, Lynn," Rob added.

"Kiss ass," Lorena called from the stoop.

Lynn half-smiled. "Thank you, both."

After they left, Rob turned a baleful stare at me. "What did your magical voodoo uncover?"

"Penny was in love with someone who had prior military service in his background," I told them. "And someone showed up at her apartment bleeding from a gash in his forearm." I pointed at the stain on the couch arm. "That's where she tried to clean up the blood."

Rob walked over and touched the stain. "How does this help us find Penny?"

"I'm not sure it does." When he sucked his teeth, I made clear my limitations. "I can only see what I see, and most of the time, what I see has nothing to do with a case, but they are pieces of a whole."

"That and five bucks will buy you a cup of coffee, but it won't get Penny found." Rob's anger was understandable. After all, he'd just been outfoxed by his aunt-in-law, who managed to destroy potential evidence right in front of his face.

"Do we want to try the car?" I asked.

"So you can snort a dangling pine tree car freshener?" Rob's question was sarcastic, but he wasn't far off-base.

"If there's one in his vehicle, that would be great. A strong odor during a time of crisis promises some very vivid scent-related emotional memories." Even so, Clark Faber had been brutally assaulted. Did I want to experience the memory? Absolutely not. If it got Penny back to her family, would I put myself in a position to see it? Yes. Yes, I would.

"Forget it," Rob said. "I would have to sign you into the impound yard, and I'm not about to try and explain your expertise to the chief. Besides, you guys have wasted my time enough tonight. And you've lost me crucial evidence that could have been used to obtain legal search warrants. I think I've had enough of your kind of help for one night."

Ezra, who'd been quiet up to this point, zipped up his jacket. "You can drop us back at the restaurant."

I arched a questioning brow at him. He gave a slight head shake, so I zipped up my coat as well. "I guess we're done then."

"No hard feelings," Rob said. "I'm sorry it didn't work out. I was hoping...."

I nodded sympathetically. "Us too. I'm sorry I couldn't get a vision that would crack the case wide open."

The truck ride back to the Oriental Palace Restaurant was deafening in its silence. Rob and Ezra had gone back to being barely cordial. As a matter of fact, Ezra had me sit in the front, and he'd climbed into the back. If Rob wanted back in with the Holden family, he was off to a poor start.

The restaurant was closed. Rob let us out by my SUV, the only vehicle left in the dark, empty parking lot. The blizzard hadn't stopped, and there was a buildup of ice and snow on my windows and around my tires.

I had a remote start on my key fob, and happily, the car purred to life.

We got in, and I turned on my seat heaters, another thing I loved about my mini-SUV. "Are we really packing it in tonight?"

Ezra met my gaze. "What do you think?"

"I think as long as Penny is out there, the snow doesn't get too awful, and we have the energy to work, we should keep trying."

A smile spread across Ezra's lips. "That's my girl."

I shook my head and smirked, "Don't you mean your cougar? Your cradle snatcher? Your Milk?"

He laughed. "Don't let Lorena get to you. She's always marched to her own drummer."

"Is her drummer Satan?"

He laughed again. "I love you."

"I love you, too," I said with a sigh.

"Good, I'm holding you to it when Aunt Lorena says more stupid stuff."

This time I laughed, and after, I kissed him. "In a way, she's done me a favor," I told him. "I wasn't sure how I would handle it if your family had a problem with our age difference, but now I know. I'm okay with it. I told you once before as long as I'm happy with you and you're happy with me, that's all that matters. Besides, for all her horribleness, Lorena is kind of hilarious."

Ezra pursed his lips, then let out a soft "pah." "I'm glad you think so. I've always found her tiresomely over-bearing and hard to be around."

The heater finally started blowing warm, and the defrost made quick work of the windshield and back glass.

"Where are we going next?" I asked Ezra.

He put his left hand on the steering wheel and shifted the SUV into reverse, then gave me a smile. "We're going to see about an impounded car."

## CHAPTER
# THIRTEEN

The temperature outside was as bitter and unpleasant as Ezra's Aunt Lorena. In other words, it had gotten even colder. According to my phone app, it was four degrees out with a windchill that made it feel like negative ten. Before dinner, I'd changed out of my tennis shoes after the parade and put on dressy, black suede boots for the occasion. They'd definitely been fashion over function, and slogging around alleys and apartment complexes all night in sub-zero conditions had turned my feet into popsicles.

While Ezra drove, I took off my boots and put my socked feet by the heated air blowing from the floor-board vents to warm them up before putting my tennis shoes back on.

I hadn't been paying attention earlier, but now that it was just the two of us, I noticed how beautiful all the lights were as we drove through town. The displays varied, including traditional Santa fare, religious manger scenes, Charlie Brown characters, polar bears and penguins, and more.

I thought about our friends and family back home. I wondered if Gilly had told Marco and Ari about her engagement yet. How would the twins react? Probably with more enthusiasm than I had. They were both in college now and well on their way to real adulthood. Their dad, Gio, who was a total prick, had a new baby daughter with a woman who had used him to hide her true self from her family. The situation had been convoluted and sad, but Marco and Ari adored their little sister.

Pippa and Jordy were enjoying their toddler J.J.'s second Christmas. The little girl was twenty-two months old and had enough eye-hand coordination to open presents this year, though, in my estimation, she was going to enjoy tearing the wrapping paper as much as she would the gifts. I took my job as her godmother very seriously and bought J.J. a Bumble Ball that was sure to delight her and the dogs and drive Pippa and Jordy nuts. I'd gotten Marco and Ari Bumble Balls for their second Christmas seventeen years ago. The toy moved, bounced, and constantly played sounds or music. In other words, it was a classic because it never failed to excite a child while simultaneously annoying a parent.

The thought made me smile.

"What's on your mind?" Ezra asked me.

"Just thinking about home," I admitted. "J.J.'s first real Christmas. Marco and Ari are adults now."

"Gilly's engagement."

I plucked at the hem of my jacket. "That too. I am happy for her. You know that, right?" I felt selfish about my melancholy.

"I know you are." He reached over and took my hand. "It's okay to want things to stay the same while also knowing that change is inevitable, and often for the better."

I gave him a fond smile. "I hit the jackpot when I found you."

He laughed and put his hand back on the steering wheel. "Don't you mean I found you?"

"I wasn't hiding very hard." I rubbed my knees. Even with the shots I got in them every six months, the cold weather was making them ache a little.

Without making a big deal out of it, Ezra said, "We can go back to the B and B and call it a night if you want."

"No, I want to keep going," I told him. "Penny might be kicking back, enjoying the spoils of her victory tonight, or she might be scared and alone with two dangerous men. If there's even a slight chance it's the second scenario, then I don't want to give up on her."

"Let's run down what we know," he said. "Clark Faber was robbed and beaten."

I picked up the thread. "Penny was possibly

abducted, and there is a reason to believe she purposefully put herself on camera."

"All of her stuff is gone from her apartment, and she left a goodbye note to her parents."

"Where do you think her clothes and her personal items went? Surely, there isn't enough room in her car for all her worldly possessions."

"Good question. If we can get on the lot, let's find out.

"Do you know what kind of car she drives?"

"It was red," he said. "I was so mad at her, that's about all I remember."

"We'll figure it out."

"Sounds right."

I continued our rundown of what we knew about the case. "I had several visions about Penny manifest. The first one was at Weston's when she spritzed herself with cologne. She was in a clinch with a guy named Jay, and they were talking about getting her son Kyle and starting a new life." I turned to Ezra. "The goodbye letter seemed to hold the same dream for her. Do you think that running away has been a plan of hers for a while? Getting her son and taking off? Maybe this is one of the things she dreams about with whoever she's dating."

"What do we know about this, Jay?"

"He's taller than her and has dark hair." I stared out the window. "Which describes a lot of men."

Ezra nodded. "It's not a lot to go on."

A horrifying thought popped into my head. "What about her son? He lives with his father, right?"

"I was living in Hillside when she lost custody to Will Tucker. The two of them weren't married but had lived together for a few years. When they split up, Penny tried to keep Will from seeing his son, going so far as to make false allegations about him to try and get him in trouble. The court awarded Will full custody after that."

"Cripes." The more I found out about Penny, the harder it was to sympathize with her. It was no wonder, even though they were close in age, that Ezra wasn't fond of her. It also explained why he had thought Penny was having an affair with Rob when we saw them together at lunch. He believed it was in her character. Regardless, I didn't have to like the woman to want her safe and at home with her family. "That's terrible."

"She's always been a little bit overzealous when it comes to matters of the heart." His gaze grew distant and wistful. "I didn't blame Will for suing her for custody. She'd tried to prevent him from being in Kyle's life to punish him for the breakup. I can't imagine how scary it would've been if Kati had tried to keep Mason from me."

"Where does Will live? If Penny is involved, he and Kyle might be in danger."

"Crap," Ezra uttered. "I didn't think about that."

"I hadn't either until about a minute ago. Between the vision and that letter, though, it seems as if Kyle had been one of the goals."

129

"Can you call Elaine?" He handed me his phone. "Her number is in my favorites."

I punched in the code to Ezra's phone. It was 0511, Mason's birthday. Ezra's starred contacts included Mason, Elaine, Reese McKay, a detective who worked in his department, Jordy, Kati, and Shawn Rafferty, my ex-husband and his boss. My number was at the top of the list, which made me smile. He was at the top of my list with Gilly and Pippa. I called Elaine, and the call was picked up by my car's Bluetooth.

"Did you find her?" Elaine asked without pleasantries.

"Hey, sis," Ezra answered. "Nope. Not yet."

"Any news at all?" she asked.

"Do you know where her ex, Will Tucker, is living now?"

"In Springfield," she said. "Why? Do you think he's involved?"

"No, but I think he should be made aware that Penny is missing and that she could possibly show up."

"We think she might want to get to Kyle," I joined in. "And if given a chance, take him on the run with her."

Elaine paused for a moment, then asked, "Do you really think Penny would try and kidnap her son?"

Ezra nodded absently. "You know she was devastated when the court removed her as the primary guardian."

"I'd like to help," Elaine told him. "But I don't have Will's number."

"But you have Rob's," Ezra told her. "Can you call him and relay the message? He can track down Will's details and get in contact with him. If you don't want to talk to Rob, I get it. Text me the number, and I'll call him myself."

She paused for a moment, then said, "No, I'll do it."

"Oh," I said. "What kind of car does Penny drive?"

"A red Ford Focus, why?"

"Just curious," Ezra said. He flashed me a quick smile. "Thanks for your help. Maybe don't mention that we asked about Penny's car." He didn't want Rob to know that we were investigating without him. "Talk soon."

"You got it. Talk soon," she agreed, then hung up.

I recognized a church with a cross display as we turned onto a street that took us west of town. "Isn't this the road to Thorny Creek Inn?"

"The impound lot is out this way. Or at least it used to be." He frowned. "It's been a while, so I'm not sure now." He took another right, going north. "There it is," he said with satisfaction. "The impound lot."

He pulled up to the gatehouse. A middle-aged woman with voluptuous curves and bright blonde hair slid the window between us open. "What can I help you, folks, with?" Her voice had a nasal twang, and her accent was from much farther south than the Ozarks.

"My friend's car was towed today, and we need to get something out of it."

"Do you have your receipt?" she asked.

"The courthouse was closed by the time we realized," Ezra said. "It won't take but a minute."

"You'll have to come back on Monday after the holidays and with a receipt," she said. "The lot is closed tomorrow and Christmas day."

I leaned across Ezra's lap to get a better look at her. Her badge displayed the name "Janine."

"Hi, Janine." I addressed her by name because, in sales, it was important for the client to feel seen. I found that was true of most people, especially those who worked in service professions. "We will be quick. In and out. I left some medicine in the glove box."

"What kind of medicine?" she asked suspiciously.

I noticed she had multiple pictures of an English Bulldog plastered all over her back wall. "It's for my dog," I lied. "She has diabetes."

The lot lady suddenly looked interested. "What kind of dog do you have?"

"A beagle." For a short period of time, I took care of a pocket beagle named Godiva until her owner got out of jail. I'd grown quite fond of the little darling and had been sad to see her go. "Her name is Godiva." I grabbed my phone and pulled up a cute picture of Godiva and me that Ari had taken, and I showed it to her to sell the lie. "She needs her medication, and with the holiday, I can't get any more until next week."

"What kind of car is it?" Janine's expression was full of sympathy and concern. "Let's make sure it's on the lot."

"Red Ford Focus," Ezra said quickly. Smart.

Janine looked at her log, then finally, she said, "It's parked in the fifth row back toward the end. You folks go on in and get what you need. It'll be our little secret."

"Merry Christmas," I told her.

"And Merry Christmas to you," she said, then closed the window between us. In a few seconds, the gates to the secured lot opened.

"That was some quick thinking." Ezra grinned at me. "You are devious."

I felt a little bad about using Godiva in my lie. "Was it too much?"

He gave me a sly look as he drove past the gate. "Only if too much means sexy as hell."

"Hah." I shook my head. "Then I guess it was too much."

# FOURTEEN

W e cruised slowly down the fifth row, looking for a red Focus and a blue Cadillac CRS. We got lucky because the two vehicles were only separated by a white pickup with the front end smashed in. Its location between the two cars indicated the wreck had happened today.

"That's a bad one," I told Ezra as we got out.

"Uh-huh." He was focused on Faber's vehicle. "It looks like the driver-side window was smashed."

I retrieved my flashlight from my purse and moved to that side of the Cadillac with him. There was police tape crisscrossed over the opening. "There's shattered glass all over in there." But it was suspiciously missing the same volume at the center of the seat. I made a face when I saw dark spatters on the back of the seat and on the interior panel of the door. "Looks like blood. You think the window was smashed in while Faber was sitting in it?"

Ezra put a gloved hand on the roof and leaned down for a better look. "Seems like it, doesn't it."

"He must've been terrified." I saw there was a stick air freshener in the vehicle's vent. The kind that releases scent as air passes through it. The warmer the air, the stronger the odor. Right now, the chilly breeze was freezing my nostrils, and I couldn't smell anything. "I need to get inside," I said. "But I don't want to compromise any evidence."

"Do you need to be in there? Or can we just grab the air freshener and take it back to the truck?"

I gave him an assessing look. "You are brilliant."

"I'm not just a pretty face," he joked. He reached in and unclipped the scent stick from the vent.

"Let's check out Penny's car before we get back in the truck." Violent and traumatic memories, unlike the happy ones, took it out of me.

Ezra understood. He pocketed the air freshener. "First the Focus."

The red car was unlocked. I assumed Penny had the key on her when she'd been in the alley. "Do you think the key we found belongs to this car?"

"It didn't look like a car key, but maybe it fits the trunk."

I reached down and hit the trunk button and heard the creak and groan under the weight of fresh snow as it opened. We walked around to the back.

"Well, I didn't expect that," Ezra said as we stared at a whole lot of nothing.

"Talk about anticlimactic," I concurred. "I wonder where her stuff is?"

"Maybe she mailed it off."

"It would be impossible to check that, though, right? I mean, she wouldn't use the post office. Maybe a moving service. Rob could check her credit cards to see if she hired anyone or maybe dropped some boxes with a delivery service."

"It would take a bit of convincing a judge, but he could get it done."

"If he will," I said. "Let me sit inside for a moment and see what I can see."

Ezra opened the car door for me, and I slid into the driver's seat. He closed it behind me, and it barely took the nip out of the cold. There weren't any air fresheners in Penny's vehicle and no obvious scents that triggered my smell-o-vision. I opened the glovebox to find paperwork, fast food napkins, and motion sickness pills. I checked the center console next. There was some hand gel, gum, leather gloves, a charging cable, and some watermelon lip balm.

I popped the cap off the tube and closed my eyes as I brought it close to my nose. The sweet essence of artificial watermelon emanated from the balm. It reminded me more of candy than a fresh, ripened melon. Still, I felt the aura of a scent memory tickle at the back of my consciousness....

A man in jeans and a flannel shirt grabs a woman's hand. They are standing outside by what looks like large garage doors. It's somewhere I don't recognize. "What are you saying?" he whispers to her. "I thought this was what you wanted. I am doing this for you."

"You're not, though, are you," she says. I recognize her voice as belonging to Penny from the previous visions. "If you were doing it for me, you'd call it off."

"He's a liar. A liar and a cheat. You know this. How could you fall for his crap? He's using you?"

"You mean the way you wanted me to use him? Like the way, you're using me? We can't even tell anyone we're together."

"You know why. It's better if we just get the money and go."

"No," she shakes her head and yanks her hand from his grip. She takes a lip balm from her purse, and while I can't see her face, I can deduce that she's applying it. "I'm done. Out. Get it. It's over. It's better if you let me go and forget about all this. Forget about me. It's not worth it." Her tone softens. "I'm not worth it."

"You are, Pen. You know I love you. I can't give you up," he pleads with her. "Just tell me how to fix this."

"We can't do this," Penny says. "You have to stop."

His pleading tone turns to venom, and he shoves her against a wall, his face moving close to hers. "You're mine, get it."

"No, Jaybird." She places her hand on his chest to hold him back. "Stop."

*He snarls, "These hips are mine." He puts a hand on her hip. "These sweet lips are mine." He kisses her. "Your life is mine." She stops fighting him.*

Whoa. When I came out of the memory, I could still feel the desperation, anger, and possessiveness captured in the scent. The emotions were definitely his, not hers. This was Jay or Jaybird's memory, not Penny's. It was the moment she'd broken his heart. I got out of the car, leaving the lip balm on the seat as I closed the door behind me. The blast of cold air was better than a splash of cold water to bring me back to the present.

Ezra waited for me to get my bearings before asking, "What did you see?"

"She tried to end it with the Jay guy. He said she was being used by a new man, and the way he tried to hold on to her...." I rubbed my arms to ward off the lingering sensations. "It was frightening."

Ezra put his arm around me. "Let's get you warmed up in the truck. Maybe we should hold off on you sniffing that scent stick until later. You look wiped."

"I feel wiped," I confessed. "But what if it elicits a vision that gives us a clue to Penny's whereabouts? Because I think one thing is certain, she doesn't want to be with this Jay guy, and if he's the one who took her, she's in danger. If she doesn't prove she wants to be with him, he's going to hurt her."

*Your life is mine*, he'd said.

I wrapped my arms around Ezra, needing warmth, needing our connection. I buried my face against his chest. "If she can't make him believe she still loves him, I'm worried he'll kill her."

"Come on." He gently patted my back. "Let's go back to the inn and regroup."

I didn't protest as he opened the passenger door for me. As we drove out, Janine waved to us from the security shack.

It didn't take long to get back to the Thorny Creek Inn, and I was glad there was parking down at the carriage house, so it was a short walk to our room. I'd been excited about walking the holiday-decorated path earlier, but the only thing I wanted for Christmas right now was a hot shower and a soft bed.

When the shower was checked off my list, I felt more myself. I wrapped my hair in a towel and put on the complimentary robe. Ezra sat in one of the rockers in front of the sliding glass doors. He'd pulled the curtain open to look at the lake. The trees around the water were strung with lights and cast reflections on a layer of ice. It was a new moon tonight, so the sky was naturally darker than normal. With everything covered in a blanket of snow, the landscape took on a blueish tinge that fit my current mood. I came up behind Ezra, leaned over, and rested my forearms on his shoulders.

He covered my hands with his. "Feeling better."

"Mmm-hmm." I kissed the top of his head before standing to my full height. "I finally feel warm again."

He gestured to a steaming cup on the small table between the rockers. "I made you some hot tea."

"Perfect." I stood up and walked around the rockers to sit in the empty one. "It's been a long day."

He grunted emphatically. "That's the understatement of understatements. It feels like we've been here a year, and this weekend has barely begun."

"I'm sorry for your family. I think your mom was really looking forward to having you home and without all the drama." I sipped my tea. It was hot and sweet. Delicious.

"My family was built on drama," he said. "It's one of the many things I love about you. You're not the kind of person who makes mountains out of molehills."

"There are enough mountains without manufacturing more," I said.

He laughed. "Exactly right."

I had put my phone on the charger when we got into the suite, and it had been close to ten when we'd arrived. I tried not to think about the vision from the watermelon lip balm. Those kinds of visions were like emotional vampires. They sucked the joy out of me. But for me, it wasn't my damage. It was Penny's trauma, and God only knew what she was going through right now. Especially if she was with this Jay fellow. Ezra had given me permission to ignore the scent stick we'd taken from Faber's car, but my own conscience was struggling with giving me the same permission. I wouldn't be able to forgive myself if I ignored it tonight, only to find out in the morning it could've saved Penny's life.

"Where'd you put it?" I held out my hand.

"Put what?"

"You know what." I gave him the stink-eye. "The car freshener."

"I wish you wouldn't," he said.

"I know." I took his hand and lifted it to my lips. I kissed the back of his fingers. "And I love that you want to protect me, but I'm not the one that needs to be saved right now. It's been over five hours since Penny went missing. I might be able to see if anyone says something about where they plan to go. They could be in another state at this point. If I can get a clue to where I need to try."

He sighed before getting to his feet. He had put the scent stick in a plastic bag that had been folded up in the ice bucket. He handed me the bag. "You don't have to do this."

I gave him a sad smile. "Yes, I do. It's the right thing." I took the stick from the plastic and wrinkled my nose. It was new car scent—a mix of leather and ozone. Yuck. I waved it close to my face and inhaled deeply....

*A man in a car locks the door, and another man with a hammer smashes the window in. Shards of glass are everywhere. The man in the car tries to get to the passenger side, but another man is waiting on that side. The driver-side door is yanked open.*

*"Give me the key, Ke-vin," the man says. I am certain the man is Clark Faber because of what Rob told us, and it feels like the man with the hammer is using the name Kevin as some kind of taunt. "I'm not going to ask twice."*

"I...I...don't..." the man in the car stammers. Before he can say more, the guy with the hammer reaches in and grabs him by the hair and drags him out into a field. It's twilight, so it's semi-dark out, and I can't make out much about the two men because the guy, Kevin, keeps closing his eyes as they slap him around the face.

"You promised not to hurt him," a woman says. It's Penny's voice again. "Give him the combination," she implores the man being abused. "They'll let you go."

"One four seven eight three seven," he quickly fires off. "The safe is in the trunk."

The man that had been on the passenger side says, "Yee-haw!" or something like that, as he reaches into the car and pops the trunk.

"Just let him go now," Penny cries.

"Not until I get everything," the hammer dude tells her. "And I mean everything." He grabs the man on the ground by the neck and says, "Where are you keeping the real loot? I know you have...." He pivots his head to Penny, "what did you tell me? Oh, yeah. A hundred grand from the life insurance. All in cash." He turns back to the man on the ground. "That's the key I want."

"Never," the downed man sputters.

"A deal's a deal," the man with the hammer says. "No money, no mercy." He addresses Penny again. "Say goodbye to your boyfriend, love." He stands to his full height and drops a booted sole onto Kevin's face.

I jerked to attention as the vision came to an abrupt halt. My hands were shaking, and I had a knot in my throat. I couldn't stop thinking about the sheer brutality of the incident. There was no hesitation to harm in the cruel man. Never had I wished so much that I could see the faces of the people in my visions.

"Nora." Ezra's voice was tight with worry. "Tell me."

"There's more money." My neck knotted as I saw the boot coming down. "And he's not going anywhere until he gets it."

"Who?"

"Jaybird." I turned my watery gaze to Ezra. "The guy who has Penny."

# FIFTEEN

*December 24<sup>th</sup>, Christmas Eve...*

The next morning, Ezra and I went to the main house of the Thorny Creek Inn to enjoy a nice drama-free breakfast. After my visions the night before, Ezra had texted Elaine, and she'd texted Rob, and Rob had called us. I relayed what I'd seen the best I could. He was angry we'd gone behind his back to the impound lot. Even so, he'd thanked me for my effort and for the information. Honestly, I didn't know how much any of what I'd seen would help the investigation. There hadn't been any clues to Penny's whereabouts in them, and that's what we needed.

My sleep had been fitful and filled with the ruthless, faceless man who'd do whatever it took to get what he wanted. Ezra had awakened me once when I'd called out in my sleep. I was so ready to put the nightmare behind me.

The long dining table in the inn had a red runner going down the center and small bough wreaths with candles as decoration on the top. Molly served us cheese and spinach quiche with crispy potatoes, two bacon strips, and a side of freshly baked buttered sourdough toast.

"This looks wonderful, Molly." I took a bite of the quiche. It was creamy and cheesy with a crisp, flaky crust. "Mmm. Delicious."

Molly beamed with pleasure at the compliment. There were two other couples at the table, Norton and Donna Hightower from St. Louis, an older couple, a husband and wife, in their seventies, and another couple, Roberta and Elsie Dixon, a wife and wife, who looked to be around my age, from Kansas. During breakfast, we found out a lot about our dining companions. Apparently, Norton and Donna had gotten engaged on Christmas at the inn in 1969. Their son, who lived in California, couldn't make it home for the holiday, so he'd paid for them to spend a week at the inn. Roberta and Elsie had met at the inn five years earlier, and their holiday stay was their date-iversary present to themselves.

When they inquired about us, Ezra said, "I wanted to introduce the love of my life to my family."

"That is so sweet," Elsie gushed. "And romantic."

"Maybe you two will get engaged for Christmas like we did," Donna suggested.

"Oh, look," I said. "It's getting late." It was getting close to ten a.m. "We better get to your parents' house. We told your mom we'd come early."

Ezra smirked. "Like a deer in headlights," he mumbled.

---

LYNN HAD her coat on and met us outside when we arrived. "Orsen and Lettie usually cook pancakes for the Christmas in Uniform Brunch at the firehouse, but since Penny's disappearance, neither of them is in any shape to be of service. I've offered our assistance."

"I'm happy to do it," I said, and I meant it. I'd take flipping flapjacks over awkward intimate conversations any day.

"Great. Can we take your car? Hal got called to the plant. The sprinkler pipes froze last night, and one of them burst. I guess they have water everywhere."

"Yikes."

Lynn nodded. "It was shooting out like a fountain, and some of the water was freezing before it could hit the ground. It looks like an ice sculpture." She opened her phone and showed us a photo. The shot had water spraying into the air, and below it was, in essence, an ice sculpture that looked like crashing waves."

"Cool."

"Not if you're the one who has to deal with it," she said. "He wasn't supposed to go back to work for at least another two weeks, but I couldn't talk the man down. I think Penny's disappearance is making him feel useless. Getting the call this morning to go to work perked him up. Fool man."

Ezra, who'd been quiet up until then, said, "What's wrong with dad?"

Lynn looked startled at the question. She shook her head. "It's not all that big of a deal."

"He's on blood thinners and strong pain pills. That sounds like a big deal."

His mother's brows knitted together. "Were you snooping in my bathroom?"

"Yes," he said without any hint of remorse. "Penny told me dad was sick but didn't tell me any more than that. I can't believe you didn't call me to let me know."

"To paraphrase a man I know, the phone goes both ways."

"We talk every week."

Neither of them was raising their voice, but that didn't stop this from being a fight. I went back and forth over whether to intervene or not.

"I talk," Lynn corrected him. "You keep your answers short, and you never ask me any questions."

"Oh, so not telling me was your way of punishing me?"

"I am not punishing you," she said. "Your dad didn't want me to say anything. He had a bowel perforation, and they were able to repair it laparoscopically without having to open him up, but he's not supposed to lift anything heavy for six weeks, in which he only has two left, and he's got to be on blood thinners until then. It's not a big deal. He only spent two days in the hospital. Oh, and he has to be on a soft diet until then, too, and it's making him and me crazy," she blurted out. "So, if there is anyone doing the punishing around here, it's you. When Kati got pregnant, I handled it badly, and I'm sorry. I thought you were throwing away your life. I shouldn't have been so shortsighted, but you're my son, and I love you. Raising a baby at sixteen is hard." Lynn was crying now. "I wanted your life to be easy. I said and did things that I'm not proud of, but, son, when are you going to forgive me?"

Ezra looked like the wind had gotten knocked out of him.

Lynn wiped her tears with the back of her gloves. She sniffled as she turned to me. "I'm sorry, Nora. This has got to be the worst Christmas ever for you."

I wasn't sure she was wrong. Between Penny's disappearance, the violent visions, and Ezra's family drama, things were going south fast. I tried to smile, but my stomach was icky with the turbulence of stress. "It's not Christmas yet," I said. "We've got some pancakes to make, right?"

"Yes." She sniffled again. "Can we take your car?"

"Yeah, sure." I widened my eyes at Ezra. He looked

numb, but he managed to turn and head to the car. "You can sit up front," I told Lynn.

She got into the backseat. Wowza.

Ezra turned on the radio, and "Wonderful Christmastime," sung by Paul McCartney, began to play. He tapped the dial and turned it off. Oh, yeah. Worst Christmas ever.

---

CHRISTMAS IN UNIFORM was an event where grateful citizens in town came out to cook and serve breakfast to all the firefighters, police officers, EMTs, and all other city employees who had to work over the holiday. It was a way to give back to the men and women who served their community. I thought the idea was cool enough that I planned on suggesting it for Garden Cove next year.

The car ride over was somber. Neither Ezra nor his mother spoke a word. Lynn had confessed her truth, and now Ezra was going to have to decide how he felt about it. It wasn't ideal timing, but feelings like burps were better to let out than keep in. Although both could be embarrassing when overheard in public.

Ezra parked the car along the road a block down from the firehouse because the parking lot and both sides of the street near the building were packed with other vehicles.

"This is quite the turnout," I mused. My innocuous observation sent a ripple through the silence.

Lynn opened her door and practically sprinted up the street ahead of us. Ezra sat still, staring out the window.

"I love you," I told him because I didn't know what else to say. Any advice I might give him would be unwelcome and most likely unhelpful.

He pursed his lips and glanced at me out of the side of his eye. "That was intense."

"Yep."

"My dad isn't dying." His grip tightened on the steering wheel, and I could see the fight in his face to hold his emotions together. I hadn't realized he'd been sitting on that fear this whole time.

"No, he isn't," I said with tenderness. "He's not dying."

Ezra nodded. He closed his eyes for a moment, and when he opened them, he took a deep breath and let it out.

"Are you okay to do this?" I asked. "We can stay, we can go back to the inn and huddle there until Monday, we can pack our stuff and go home. Whatever you want, I'm down for it."

The corner of his mouth tugged up, and my heart skipped a beat. Progress.

He gave a slight shrug. "We're here. We might as well make pancakes."

"Might as well," I agreed.

We got out of the car and strolled up the street to the firehouse.

It was crazy crowded. Lots of men and women in uniforms sat at long buffet tables with white tablecloths and Christmas adornments, chatting and laughing with each other. Several large propane heaters blasted warm air, managing to make the open space bearable. A host of volunteers manned four giant griddles, each of them at least four or five feet wide. Beyond that was food warmers that held bacon, sausage patties, scrambled eggs, and hashbrowns. At the very end was a butter and syrup station.

"This is very well organized," I said. "I'm impressed."

"I wonder how long they've been doing it." Ezra guided us past several tables toward the cook and service area. "They weren't doing this when I lived here."

On the line was several of Ezra's relatives, including Elaine, Baxter, Rose Marie, and.... I inwardly groaned but outwardly smiled, Lorena. I hoped she'd forgotten to put her shrew hat on this morning.

"Hi," Rose Marie said cheerily. "It's so nice to see you again." She shook her head. "Just terrible about Penny."

"It is." I looked around. "Where do you want me?"

"Somewhere out of town would be a good start," Lorena goaded.

I coughed as the comment took me off guard. "Good morning to you too, Lorena."

She grumbled something that I actively ignored.

Fortunately, the scent of breakfast foods only elicited happy memories from the crowd. Yay.

Elaine walked over to us and said, "You guys want to help me serve the stuff from the warmers?"

"Mmm, mmm," Ezra teased. "Stuff sounds so appetizing."

Elaine poked him in the ribs. "Smart alec."

"Mom told me about dad's surgery," he said casually to her, but I knew he was feeling anything but casual.

Elaine winced. "Yeah, sorry about that. Dad made me swear not to tell you. He wanted you home for Christmas, not because he was a sick old man." She nudged her brother. "Besides, if it had been really serious, you know I would have broken that promise so fast I'd have gotten whiplash." She smiled at him. "So don't be mad, okay?"

"Okay." He gestured toward the rows of tables. "When did all this start?"

"When Rollo became a fireman about five years ago," his sister said. "Aunt Lettie got upset that he had to work over the holiday, and she organized this whole thing so that she could spend time with her *wittle boy* on Christmas eve." Elaine laughed. "Baxter is a fireman, too," she added. "But he's off today, so he's manning the line with us."

"I think it's genius," I told her. "Every town should do something like this."

Lynn had taken a position near her sister, and she

kept her head down as she poured circles of batter on the hot surface.

"What's wrong with Mom?" Elaine asked.

Ezra shrugged, which was the only answer his sister was going to get.

"Fine," she said. "Rob told me you all found a key in the alley last night. Do you really think it was Penny's way of trying to send a message? She's clever, I'll give her that. And she can manipulate with the best of them, but she's never been particularly smart." Elaine said that last bit quietly.

Rollo came up to our section with two other men. I recognized the guy with the equine nose even out of his Santa outfit. "Howdy, Howdy." I shook my head with chagrin. "Sorry. I can't seem to help myself."

He laughed. "I don't mind."

The other guy said, "I'm Blake. We met too." Without the Santa beard, I saw that Blake had a cherry birthmark on his cheek. My grandmother used to call them angel kisses.

"Good to see you again, Blake." I nodded. "I'll remember you next time. Promise."

Rollo asked, "Do you all know if Rob is any closer to finding Penny?" He scrubbed his face. He had a day's worth of stubble, and his eyes were red with exhaustion. "I drove around all night hoping to find her."

"I'm sorry," Ezra told him. "We came up empty."

"Except for a key," Elaine told him. "Do you know

why she'd think it was important enough to keep it away from whoever she's with?"

Ezra shot his sister a loose-lips-sink-ships look.

She blanched. "Or, you know, whatever."

Rollo shook his head. "Mom told me about the letter. She's devastated."

Now it was Elaine's turn to shoot Ezra a what-am-I-missing look.

He ignored her. "Try to hold onto hope, bud. The police are doing everything they can to bring her home safe."

After Rollo and his buddies moved down the line, I asked Elaine, "Where're the girls?"

"They're with Rob's parents this morning to open presents with them. I'm picking them up later."

"Must be hard," I sympathized.

"It has been."

Someone waved at Ezra from across the room. He gave me a kiss on the temple and said, "Be right back."

"He's so in love with you," Elaine commented as she plopped a spoonful of eggs onto a police officer's tray. "I've never seen him so content."

"He makes me happy, too."

"Rob and I used to be like that." She heaved a wistful sigh. "Two babies later, and contentment went right out the window."

"What happened with you two? If you don't mind me asking."

"I don't mind. It started with a little bickering...then

a lot of bickering, and then finally, we moved into the completely-ignore-each-other phase. I guess I shouldn't have been surprised when Rob suggested we take some time apart. I felt blindsided and betrayed." She tossed the metal spoon back into the eggs. "So I told him that if he wanted to take some time, he'd get it, as in forever time. It got messy quick from there."

"It sounds like it." I used tongs to move two pieces of bacon onto another officer's plate.

"Thanks," he muttered. I looked up and saw it was Officer Rogers, the cop who'd threatened to taser Ezra. He didn't look any happier than he had the day before.

"Have a nice day," I said, then turned my attention back to my conversation with Elaine. "For what it's worth, and that's probably not much. I think Rob is still in love with you."

She peered at me. "That ship has sailed. I missed my opportunity to fix our marriage when he'd brought up a temporary split."

"I don't know about that." I tapped my nose. "Just saying."

"When I talked to Rob last night, you know, for Ezra about Penny, it reminded me so much of when we were first together. He used to tell me about his work, and we'd talk for hours. Last night was the first time we'd talked like that in years." Elaine's shoulders slumped. "The girls are finally adjusting to our new situation. I can't allow myself to get my hopes up. I won't put them through more pain." She tilted her chin back and met my gaze. "So, this...ability of yours. It's real, right?"

"Real enough." So real it haunted my dreams.

"How does it work?" She absently rubbed the base of her naked ring finger. "I mean, do you touch something and get a glimpse of the future."

"Oh." It dawned on me why she was asking. "I'm not that kind of psychic. I'm sorry, Elaine. I don't see the future. Only memories of the past, and only how it's related to scents."

Her face bunched. "How does that work?"

We were by ourselves at the end, and our conversation was quiet, so I didn't mind answering the question. "If someone has an emotional memory that is triggered by a scent, like, say, the perfume of jasmine brings up a memory of you and your mother pruning a jasmine bush that's in bloom, then I would see that memory."

I stared down the line at Lynn. Ezra's memory had held so much love that I knew still existed between them if they could let go of the past to see it.

"Mom loves jasmine," Elaine said.

I continued my explanation without getting more into Ezra's memory of a less complicated time. "I've been trying to get better at finding specific memories while blocking others. It's hit-and-miss. If I can tie one of my own memories to an aroma, it helps in the blocking department. A friend of mine was in trouble once, and she used a tube of eucalyptus and mint lip balm to leave me a memory of who had kidnapped her and that she was in the trunk of his car."

"Wild," Elaine whispered. "That was the case with the mayor of your town, right? The one that I read about on Stupor."

I nodded. "That would be the one."

"Amazing." Elaine's eyes were full of wonder, and her posture was upright again. I was glad I'd been able to take her mind off her troubles.

Howdy came back for a second scoop of potatoes and a sausage patty.

I had to fight the urge to call out, "How-dee!" But I managed. Barely.

Ezra walked back over. "That was a guy I knew from high school. He's an EMT now."

I smiled. "Nice."

Lorena came over and stared Ezra down.

"Can I help you with something, Aunt Lorena?" he asked.

"Yeah," she said tersely. "You can stop being a butt-hole who breaks his mother's heart." She didn't wait for his response, which was probably good because I had a feeling she'd be waiting until the grave.

"That woman has zero boundaries," I muttered.

Elaine hawed. "I think that's the nicest way I've ever heard someone call Aunt Lorena a bitch."

At my side, Ezra began humming, "Wonderful Christmastime."

## CHAPTER
# SIXTEEN

The brunch went off without any more major drama. Lynn caught a ride home with Lorena and Rose Marie. I thought she was still upset about her fight with Ezra and maybe even a little embarrassed. Lynn, Lorena, and Lettie were supposed to be preparing Christmas dinner this afternoon, but since Lettie had canceled, Rose Marie had stepped up to take her place.

"How can I help?" I'd asked when the subject came up. Lorena had a few choice suggestions. Lynn told her about a high cliff where she could take a flying leap.

"I'd love for you to join us, Nora," Lynn told me. She stuck her tongue out at her older sister. "Why don't you and Ezra come over around two o'clock. He can help Hal run errands while we take care of kitchen duty."

I knew without looking that Ezra was trying not to laugh. However, I wasn't a complete flop in the kitchen. I could totally reheat restaurant leftovers without burning them, and I wasn't terrible at cutting up vegetables. I did it for Gilly sometimes when she made big meals.

When Ezra and I were alone in the car, I asked, "We have two hours. What would you like to do?"

The grin on his face was ear-splitting.

Normally, I would be completely on board for a little holiday cheer, but I was still tired from the night before. "Only if it involves a nap."

Ezra winked. "I'll be quick."

I didn't believe him for a minute. "I was thinking more along the lines of going to the hospital in Springfield and checking in on Clark Faber."

"It sounds like a lot less fun," he said. "But if that's what you want, then let's do it. I haven't been to Springfield in a long time. He's probably not awake. What are you thinking?"

"I still feel out of sorts from the vision last night, and I feel like I won't be able to shake it until I see the man."

"Fair enough," he said. "It's as good a reason as any. And while we're in Springfield, I'll drive you past some of my old stomping grounds."

"I'm sure I will be suitably impressed."

Ezra grinned. "Keep your expectations low."

"With you? Never." I scoffed. "You haven't disappointed me yet."

We exited Hillside and turned south onto MO-13.

After all the snow we'd had the day before, the roads were remarkably clear. There was a green city and mile sign that said *Springfield 13*.

"Did you stay in Hillside when you worked for the police department in Springfield?" I asked. He didn't talk much about his work before Garden Cove. Every once in a while, a case would remind him of an old one, but otherwise, Ezra was the kind of man who lived in the present, except when it came to his mother, obviously.

"I lived in an apartment complex south of town," he said. "The Oak Apartments on Lamonte street." He tucked his chin. "Remarkably, it looked a lot like Penny's place. A basic shoe box with a kitchen and a bathroom." He scratched his neck, and I was fascinated by the way his Adam's apple bobbed up and down while he recollected his past. "But it was plenty for me. I had a sofa bed that I slept on when I had Mason, so he could sleep in the bedroom." He lifted his fingers from the steering wheel and gestured with them as he spoke. "I was always worried that he was going to get up and walk out if I didn't stand guard between him and the front door." His expression grew worried. "Aunt Lettie and Uncle Orsen have to be losing their minds right now."

"Did you call Mason today?" I asked.

"Yes," he admitted. "When you were in the shower this morning. I needed to hear his voice and make sure he was doing okay. And he is. He's spending the day at Portman's on the Lake with Kati, Roger, Allie, and Claire."

Claire Portman, Kati's mother-in-law, had moved into a suite at the resort a few months after her husband went to prison. He'd been part of a group of business owners in Garden Cove who had been running their own crime syndicate. The resort had been in Claire's name, and she'd been completely cleared of having any knowledge about her husband's shady dealings. Truthfully, I thought she was much happier without him, and she loved living at the resort where she didn't have to do any of her own cooking or cleaning.

"I'm sure Mason is having a good time but missing you."

"He says Allie is starting to talk in complete sentences," Ezra mused. "He's completely in love with her."

Allie was Mason's new baby sister. Kati and Roger had adopted her from India about two and a half years ago. The little girl had completed their family.

"I know you miss him."

"I'll see him next week." His voice was calm and reasonable sounding, but I could tell I'd hit the nail on the head. "My argument with Mom this morning brought up a lot for me. It reminded me of why I try so hard to be there for Mason however he needs me."

"And you've been a great dad."

Ezra's lips thinned. "He's made the job easy." I heard the unspoken, *unlike me.*

"Hey now, I really like the guy you're beating up on."

I reached over and rubbed the back of his neck for a few seconds. "I think you should give him a break."

"Mom struck a nerve, is all."

"I get it. But don't let one fight undo what you know is true about yourself."

"What's that?"

"You're a good and honorable man who always tries to do the right thing, even when it's not easy." I chuckled as a thought struck me. "For a guy nicknamed Easy, you sure are hard on yourself sometimes."

The dimples in his cheeks deepened as he smiled. "Baby, isn't that the truth."

---

DOZENS OF TUBES and wires protruded from the unconscious man in the hospital bed. His head was bandaged, and his face was bruised and swollen. The I.C.U. nurse had told us that, since we weren't immediate family, we weren't allowed in the room, but the door was open, and they hadn't kicked us out.

"His own mother wouldn't recognize him," Ezra whispered. "I can't believe he survived."

From what Lynn had said, Faber's mother had suffered from Alzheimer's before she died. I wondered how often she'd recognized him when he hadn't been battered. I pushed the uncomfortable and insensitive thought from my head. The man had given up his military career and took early retirement to come home and be with her for her final days. His actions made me feel as if I knew him a little bit. After all, I'd practically done the same thing when I gave up my career to take care of my mother.

"Ezra?" I heard someone say. "Hey, it is you. Ezra Holden."

A large, older black man with short, gray hair moved quickly in our direction. He wore a light gray uniform and a hospital security badge.

Ezra blinked. "Sergeant Davis?"

"Dang, son," the older officer said with a smile. "Good to see you. Are you here visiting someone?"

"Yep." Ezra indicated Faber's room with a tilt of his head. He shook the older man's hand. "What are you doing here?" He looked genuinely pleased to see Davis.

"I work here. I'm the head of hospital security now. I did my thirty years at S.P.D., but I couldn't sit at home. You know me. I need something to do."

"That's great," Ezra said. He put his hand on my back and said, "Sergeant Davis, I'd like you to meet my partner, Nora Black. Nora, meet my training officer from my rookie days, Sergeant Grady Davis."

"Partner?" he asked with mild surprise. "You on the job, Nora?"

I snickered. We were really going to have to come up with a different term to describe our relationship. "Somedays, it certainly feels like it."

He squinted at me and said, "Huh?"

"I'm not a police officer," I told him. "I'm Ezra's...." I used a term that made me cringe. "Girlfriend."

Davis's eyes widened, and his grin went toothy. "Well, I'll be. You're punching above your weight these days," he told Ezra.

"I don't disagree," my guy said. "I've been outclassed since the day we met."

I'll admit, I was a little flattered by the attention. After two days of Lorena's cougar jibes, it was nice to have someone think I was a prize worth keeping.

"Any who," Davis said. "Where did you move to again? How are you doing? And that son of yours.... He must be, oh, seventeen or eighteen now."

"Nineteen," Ezra said when his training officer took a breath. "I moved to Garden Cove, and I'm doing really good there. I'm the supervising detective over the special investigations team."

"Impressive," Davis said with pride. "I knew you'd go far. You were always smart."

"He went undercover on a joint task force with the F.B.I. and the D.E.A. this past year," I bragged. His efforts had injected the Garden Cove P.D. with a huge payday, and I was proud of the work he'd done in taking down a drug trafficking ring. "The operation seized millions of dollars in operating cash and drugs, along with making dozens of arrests to get some major dirtbags off the streets."

"Even more impressive." Davis's smile warmed me. He nodded to Ezra. "What are you doing back in these parts? Your family's from around here, right? No one's sick, I hope."

"Just up the road in Hillside," Ezra said. "They're home and healthy."

Mostly, I thought. Penny was missing, and Hal was recovering from surgery. But that wasn't my business to tell.

"We've come to check on Clark Faber." Ezra pointed to Faber's room. "He was brought in yesterday. A robbery and assault victim."

"Are you working the case?" Davis asked.

"No, sir," Ezra replied. "My cousin Penny has been abducted, and the attack on Faber is connected."

The old officer whistled. "I'm sorry to hear about your cousin." He raised a brow. "Hold on a minute." He took a smartphone from his utility belt. "Everything is electronic these days. Even records. I have access to whatever we might've sent to the police. What did you say his name was?"

"Clark Faber," I supplied.

"C. L. A. R. K," Davis said as he typed on the tiny keyboard. "F. A. Ope, there he is." He gave a firm nod. "Faber, Clark. Thirty-nine-year-old white male brought in at six-thirty-eight with substantial head trauma." He made a face. "Yikes. They had to drill a hole in his skull to relieve pressure from a brain bleed. Someone must've really hated him to beat him like that." The older officer walked over to the room's open door. He whistled. "Sure wouldn't recognize him the way he looks now. He doesn't look anything like his picture."

"You have a picture of him?" I asked. I was desperate to put a face to the blurred man in my vision. "Can I see?"

"It's an old scan of his driver's license," Davis said. "It was on file from when he was in the hospital for a C.T. a few years ago."

He used his forefinger and thumb to widen the picture on the screen. The scan had been black and white. Faber's photo showed an average-looking man with short hair, a square jaw-line and a smallish nose. He wasn't handsome, but he also wasn't unattractive. And yesterday evening, he'd been beaten within an inch of his life because of another man's jealousy. A shiver went up my spine as I remembered his fear.

I closed my eyes for a moment.

"Are you okay, Nora?" Davis asked. "Do you need to sit down?"

I opened my eyes and shook my head. "Thank you, Sergeant Davis."

"You can call me Grady, please. Any friend of Ezra's is a friend of mine."

There was nothing else we could do at the hospital, and with gratitude to Grady, we'd gotten more information than I'd expected. With a hand shake and a hug, we left the hospital.

"I liked your friend," I told Ezra as we crossed the parking lot.

"He taught me a lot when I came out of the academy. He was one of the best cops I've ever worked with." Ezra's phone rang. He frowned. "It's Rob."

Had they found Penny? Was she alive? Or had the outcome turned tragic? I held my breath, afraid of bad news.

Ezra put the speaker on and answered with a "You're on with Nora and me."

"Have you seen Elaine?" Rob asked.

"She was at the pancake brunch with us until noon," I said.

"Have you heard from her since then?"

I put my hand on Ezra's arm. He shook his head.

"She said she was going to pick the girls up from your parents' house and take them over to Mom and Dad's place," Ezra said.

"She never showed up for the kids." Rob's voice was tight with worry. "And she's not answering her phone."

"Maybe she's not answering because it's you," Ezra replied, not with anger, but with any safe reason that would have allowed Elaine to ignore his calls. "I'll give her a try and call you back." He hung up and tapped Elaine's name on his favorite's list. "I'm sure it's nothing," he assured me, not sounding so sure. "She's probably doing some last-minute shopping and left her phone in the car."

"Probably," I agreed, but I couldn't keep the knot in my gut from forming as the call went straight to voicemail.

Ezra called Rob right back. "We'll be in Hillside in twenty minutes. Meet me at my parents' house."

"We'll find her," I told Ezra. "I believe that."

His expression made my stomach tighten to the point of pain. Christmas was turning out to be a crapfest of epic proportions.

He nodded jerkily. "Even if I have to knock on every door and turn over every stone in Hillside."

# CHAPTER
## SEVENTEEN

Ezra raced as safely as the roads would allow. There were a few slick spots once we entered Hillside that warranted more caution. He had a white-knuckled grip on the steering wheel, and I could see his thoughts spinning out of control.

"She's okay, right? This is nothing. Penny's disappearance has us all a little jumpy, right?" His voice was flat, and the questions were almost redundant.

"Hopefully, we'll know soon enough," I told him. The chances were good that Elaine was shopping like Ezra had speculated, but I didn't want to be the one to disappoint him if I was wrong. Besides, platitudes and blind assurances were not genuine comforts, so I avoided them when at all possible.

When we pulled up to his parent's house, Rob's truck was out front. And there were two vehicles in the driveway, including Hal's old pickup.

Rob sat inside his truck with his head down as white exhaust billowed from the back.

Ezra tapped on the window. Rob's head snapped up, and he turned a worried stare at us. He shut off the engine and opened the door.

"Why didn't you wait inside?" Ezra asked.

"I couldn't," Rob told him. "I can't face them until I know where she is."

Even Ezra looked reluctant, as well. Lynn would be out of her mind with worry, and Lorena, from what I'd experienced, was not the calm in a storm. Lynn needed Ezra right now, and in my heart, I thought he needed her too.

"Let's get out of the cold." I looped my arm with Ezra's. "We'll all face them together."

Rob trailed behind us as we went inside.

Lynn and Hal were sitting on the couch. Rose Marie was on her phone, and Lorena was in the chair opposite her sister.

"Cripes," the battle-axe said. "What took you so long?" She was addressing Rob, but I felt like she'd taken a wide shot that also included Ezra and me.

"Has Elaine called?" Rob asked hopefully.

Lorena snapped. "Sure, can't you see we're just all jumping for joy around here?"

"You're not helping," Lynn told her sister flatly. "Be civil or go home. I can't take any more of your sarcasm. Not right now."

Lorena's mouth puckered, but she kept it closed.

Rose Marie set her phone down. "I put out an alert on the Neighborhood's app. If someone spots her, I'll get an alert."

"She's not a lost dog," Lorena quipped, then quickly backpedaled when she caught her daughter's rueful stare. "I know you're just trying to help."

Rose Marie, who was in her early forties, preened and took an almost child-like pleasure in her mother's approval. It made me wonder if there was more reason for her mom being critical of the men in Rose Marie's life than Lorena's normal let's-make-everyone-miserable schtick.

Hal put his arm around Lynn's shoulder. "Can't you just track her phone?" he asked Rob.

"She took the app off her phone after we split up," Rob answered. "I contacted the cell phone carrier, and they said without cause, they won't track it, and no judge is going to give me a warrant because my wife's been missing an hour. But you all know this isn't like her. If Elaine says she's going to do something, she does it." He rubbed his eyes. He'd found out the hard way when she'd asked him for a divorce. "She called Mom at noon and told her she was on her way over. It should've taken her less than four minutes to get from the fire station to Olive Street. If she had made a detour, she would've called." His voice had hitched up an octave as he continued, "I've driven every road in town. She's not in Hillside, and I don't know where she is. I'm so sorry. This is all my fault. If I hadn't...."

Lynn stood up, her voice calm. "If you hadn't what? This isn't your fault any more than it is anyone else's. Elaine will show up," she said, pressing her hand over her heart. "I feel it."

Lorena gave me a look that told me she feared the worst for her niece and her sister. Still, she went to Lynn and put her hand on her back. "She'll be home before you know it."

"We're all getting worked up for nothing." Hal stood up and threw his arm up and back for emphasis. "This Penny situation has got us all paranoid. Elaine is fine. We just saw her less than two hours ago. Just wait. She's going to show up at any minute." He stared at the door, and there was something about his conviction that made everyone look as well.

After a few seconds, Lynn said, "Hal, you're bleeding."

He looked down at his hand and muttered a few cuss words. "I must've smacked the frame." He pointed to the opening between the kitchen and the living room, then pressed and used his non-bleeding hand to put pressure on the lacerated thumb. "It's nothing. No big deal."

"You're on blood thinners," Lynn scolded. "Any bleeding is a big deal. Don't make me worry about you too." She pointed to the kitchen. "Go get it under water and wash the blood off your hand. I'll get the styptic powder from the medicine cabinet."

Hal grimaced at his wife's orders but didn't argue. I could see where Ezra got his smarts.

A metallic voice sounded from a radio on Rob's belt. "Detective Phillips, please call dispatch."

Rob took his phone from his jacket pocket and dialed the station. "This is Detective Phillips for dispatch." His cheeks paled, and his frown deepened. "Are you sure?" He made his right hand into a fist. "No. Okay. Thank you. Have the officers there secure the scene. I'll be right there." He hung up the phone. His skin had gone almost bloodless.

We all waited expectantly. Even Hal and Lynn had come back into the living room with Hal's thumb bandaged with enough material to look like the top of a snowman.

"Did they find her?" Rose Marie asked.

"They found her car," Rob told us. "It's down the side of a ravine on the other side of Thorny Creek."

"Where the B and B is?" I asked.

"A few miles past," Rob said.

"What about Elaine?" Lynn's voice cracked. "Where's my girl?"

"Fire and rescue are there. They can't find her. She's not with the car."

Lorena strode to the coat rack and grabbed her purse and jacket. She looked back at all of us. "What are we waiting for?"

"You all can't go out there," Rob said.

"The hell if we can't," Lynn told him. "Hal, get your coat. We're going."

Rob gave Ezra an imploring look.

Ezra shrugged. "Sorry, but I'm with them on this one."

---

We all took separate vehicles to the scene. I thought it had been a tactical move so that no one got stuck with Aunt Lorena. Thorny Creek, it turned out, wasn't actually near the B and B that had been named for it. It was, as Rob had said, farther out. We'd passed a few nice houses on the winding, hilly road and some that were more shacks than homes.

Before long, we came upon a scene with a fire truck, an ambulance, and two police cruisers. Officer Rogers was one of the police officers directing traffic around the area. There wasn't a lot of space off the shoulder to park, and I questioned the folly of us driving four vehicles to a car wreck.

Rob and Ezra got parked first, and as Rob got out of his truck, we exited my SUV. Rollo spotted us and came trotting over. "Easy," he said. "Elaine's not down there. The driver's door is open, and it looks like she got out."

The lines around Ezra's eyes softened. Rob let out a ragged breath. "We need to get dogs in the woods down there searching for her."

Rollo nodded. "They're coming. We found some blood on the dashboard, so if she hit her head, she could be wandering around confused."

"How far could she have gotten?" Lorena asked. "With a head injury, I mean?"

Lynn, Hal, and Rose Marie were right behind her, eager to hear the answer.

Rollo shook his head and whistled and waved for another firefighter to come over. "Howdy's our search and rescue expert. He'll be able to answer your questions better than me."

The lanky man jogged over to us, his hand on his radio. "Yeah?" he said to Rollo.

"Can you answer a few questions for my family?" Rollo asked.

"You betcha." Howdy gave us a quick two-finger salute. "Whatever you folks need."

"How far could she have gotten?" Lynn asked.

"It depends on which direction she wandered. The snow is powder, and with the wind kicked up, there are no tracks to follow. We're waiting on a dog to get her scent, but exposure to the elements, hypothermia and frostbite is a real concern."

I appreciated his laying out of the information. No bull, just the facts. "She's been missing for over an hour, almost two. How long do you think she can last?"

"I don't want to speculate, ma'am," he said.

Rob's phone began to beep. He fumbled it from his pocket. "Unknown number." He tapped the green button to answer. "Detective Phillips," he relayed to the caller, followed with an "Uh-huh." His expression went stony. "I see." His eyes filled with anger and distress. He nodded. "I understand."

Ezra gave him a "what?" look.

Rob slowly shook his head. "Let me talk to her," he demanded. "Or no deal."

His anger turned to anguish. "Elaine. Elaine, honey. Are you alright?"

"I'll do it," Rob told the caller. "But I swear if you harm her...." The person on the other end must've hung up because Rob's hand dropped to his side, and the phone bounced on the easement. He focused, his grief palpable when he told Lynn and Hal. "She's alive," he informed them. "And I promise, I'm going to do whatever I have to do to get her back."

My chest squeezed as the air rushed from me. I grabbed Ezra's hand to lend him what little strength I could muster. Yesterday, we'd been looking for his cousin—a practical stranger, but today, the case had become all too personal.

Elaine, like Penny, had been taken.

# EIGHTEEN

"Not here," Ezra ordered in a hushed tone. He grabbed Rob by the arm and yanked him down the road out of earshot of the first responders.

I followed, and so did everyone else, including Rollo and Howdy.

"I need you all to step back for a moment," Rob said. "Let me talk to Ezra alone."

"No," Lynn refused. "You tell me what's going on right this moment, or I swear I'll flag down that young man directing traffic and tell him that my daughter is in danger and you're hiding information."

"Don't do that." Rob's cheeks puffed out. On a ragged breath, he hissed, "If anyone finds out, he's going to kill Elaine. He made that perfectly clear."

Lynn grabbed Hal's arm, and he pulled her close, bracing her against his body. Lorena lost her usual bluster, and Rose Marie seemed confused.

When Officer Rogers took note of us and started in our direction, Howdy said, "I'll take care of him. Whatever you guys need. Rollo is like a brother to me. That makes you all family."

With Howdy away from the group, Rob was more forthcoming. "He wants the key we found in the alley. He said he'd exchange Elaine for it. But if he gets one hint of a double cross or other police involved, he said he would...." Rob jammed his hands in his pockets. "The key is in evidence, but I can get it. I'm supposed to wait for his next call in an hour, and he'll tell me where to drop the key. Only when he gets it will he let Elaine go."

"You could lose your job," Rollo told him. "You could get arrested."

"I'd go to jail to save her," Rob declared. "I'd die for her." He raked the group with a hard gaze. "But you have to stay out of my way. No one can know about this. No one." He landed on Rollo. "I need you and Howdy to make sure the search continues, just for a short while. I need all eyes off me until this is over."

I wasn't sure going deep off the book was the right call, but I'd seen what the bad guy had done to Clark Faber. He was vicious and brutal, and I didn't think he would hesitate to follow through with his threat against Elaine.

"Did he say anything about Penny?" Rollo asked, clearly worried for her. "I know she's had her issues, and a lot of them she's brought on herself, but she's still my sister."

"I'll do everything to get them both home," Rob said. "That's a promise. But I need your help to do it."

Rollo nodded. "Howdy and I will keep the focus off you for as long as we can but call me if you need muscle. We'll back you up."

Rob gripped Rollo's upper arm. "Thanks."

Ezra looked at his parents and his aunt. "You guys should go home and wait. I'll call you as soon as we have Elaine."

"This doesn't feel right," Lynn said. "This kind of thing doesn't happen. Not to people like Elaine." She worried her lower lip between her teeth. "I can't do nothing."

"You aren't doing nothing," Ezra assured her. "You're protecting her by giving us space to get her back."

"In other words," Lorena remarked. "You want us out of the way."

"In a nutshell," Ezra affirmed. "If the person who has her gets spooked, there's no telling what he'll do. He was willing to run her off the road without any regard for her safety. It stands to reason that he'll make good on his threat if provoked."

I knew laying out the facts without mincing words about the danger Elaine was in cost Ezra.

"What about you?" Lorena pinned me with a stare. "Don't you have a set of skills or some nonsense?"

"Some nonsense," I mumbled. I didn't know how my gift could possibly help Elaine. This felt like an unplanned kidnapping. There wasn't any memory that could help with something that was impromptu. And if it was a new plan, then why? "Wait? How did this guy know about the key we found? Who did you tell?"

"No one," Rob defended himself. "I logged it into evidence last night, but I haven't even filled out my report yet."

"You told Elaine," I said.

Rollo nodded. "I heard her talking to you at brunch today about it."

"Which means others could've overheard her talking about it," Ezra added. "Wait." His brow furrowed. "Does this mean it's someone in uniform?"

My eye went to taser-happy Officer Rogers. If he hadn't been here directing traffic, he would've been my number one suspect.

"We can't jump to any conclusions, but it's a good thing to keep in mind." Rob's frown deepened. "If he's a cop, it means he'll know our tactics."

"And he'll know if the police are contacted." I sighed. This was going from bad to nuclear fast.

"They let you talk to Elaine?" Ezra asked.

Rob nodded. "Briefly." He winced. "I think she must have a head wound because she sounded confused."

"What did she say?"

"She said something about lotion." He anxiously shuffled his feet. "Look, we can keep talking about this or I can go get my wife back."

"Go get your wife," Lynn cut in. "Go get her now."

"Wait," an inkling of an idea trickled in. "What exactly did she say?"

"Every second we waste puts her in more danger," Rob protested harshly. "Let it go."

"No," I argued. "It's important. What did she say exactly?"

"The lotion, she said the lotion is everywhere." He let out a frustrated growl. "I told you it doesn't make sense."

"Hey," Rollo interjected. "When we got down to the car, there was a tube of hand lotion squeezed out all over the console and seat. The stuff was everywhere. It's smelled like one of those Yankee Candle stores."

I grabbed Ezra's hand.

He looked at me. "You think you can?"

"I think Elaine thinks I can." I gave him a meaningful look. "I told her about when Pippa was kidnapped."

"The eucalyptus and mint balm." Ezra turned to Rollo. "I'm going to need you to get me a sample of that lotion."

Rollo looked extremely confused, but he nodded. "I got it all over my climbing gear," he said. "I'll be right back."

Rob studied me. "You think Elaine left you a trail to follow."

"Maybe," I said. My entire body tingled with both hope and dread. "I can't promise anything, but maybe."

"What kind of trail?" Lorena asked suspiciously.

"The kind that only Nora can find," Ezra replied,

daring her to say another word. "Now, you all go home. I promise to call the minute I know anything."

Hal put his foot down when Lorena started to protest. "Ezra and Rob know what they're doing, and if the only way we can keep Elaine safe is by getting the heck out of the way, then that's exactly what we're going to do." He leaned close to Ezra and spoke in a hushed voice. "Don't let me down, son."

"No, sir," Ezra said. "I won't."

---

ROLLO RETURNED in short order with a pair of insulated, tan canvas coveralls. There was a dark smear on the hip and the sleeve. "That's where I got creamed," he said. "What else can I do?"

"You're doing it," Ezra replied. "And I can't thank you enough. We just need a minute, if that's okay."

"Sure." Rollo handed him the coveralls. "If you need me, holler."

After Rollo walked away, Ezra asked me, "Are you ready?"

The last two visions with this guy had been powerful and awful, like nothing I'd experienced. I'd had visions of killers that had made me puke, but none of them lingered like the ones with this guy. He felt like a textbook sociopath, with no regard for anyone but himself. I believed with all my heart, given a chance, he would kill Elaine. As for Penny, I worried he wouldn't kill her, but he would make her wish she was dead. "Ready," I told Ezra.

Rob hadn't said a word. I thought he was still skeptical but willing to grab onto any lifeline, even if it wasn't tethered to anything.

I hoped I was right. I hoped that Elaine had managed to send me a message. I tentatively took the coveralls and held the sleeve under my nose.

Lavender, vanilla, and tangerine. The combination reminded me of an Orange Creamsicle with a floral base. I concentrated on Elaine, inhaled deeply, and allowed the aroma to really penetrate my senses.

*I instantly recognize the ugly sweater and the dark blonde hair of the woman in the car. It's definitely Elaine. She groans as she pushes herself back from the deployed airbag. She's dazed but reaches to her right and feels around until she finds a large tube of hand and body lotion.*

*"Nora, I hope you get this," she mutters, then chuckles. "I'm losing my mind." She squirts half the tube and spreads it around as much as she can. "A black SUV drove me off the road," she says. "My left wrist feels broken. I can't open the door to get out of the car."*

*A man yanks the driver door open, and for the briefest of moments, Elaine feels rescued. He's wearing tan coveralls and a black ski mask, and he has his hood up.*

*"No, no," she protests.*

*He has a gun. "Get out of the car," he demands.*

*"What do you want from me?" She sounds like she's crying.*

*"I want the key to Faber's safe room," he says. "And you're my price of admission."*

*"Clark Faber?" Elaine asks.*

*He grabs her by the arm, and her wrist snaps. She screams, but he doesn't care. He yanks her out and onto the ground. "Climb."*

My knees buckled as the vision faded. Ezra kept me from collapsing to the ground as I sipped the cold air so it wouldn't choke me.

"Did she leave you a clue?" Rob asked, no longer on the fence about me. "What did you see?"

"Faber," I gasped. "The key belongs to Faber. He wants it to open a safe room in the house."

"Faber?" Rob asked. "He's in the hospital."

I shook my head. "The kidnapper. He wants whatever is in that room." I ran my hands over the tan coveralls in my grasp.

"Rob, are these coveralls standard issue for city workers in Hillside?"

He nodded. "Everyone gets a pair for severe cold weather. I have a pair in the back of my truck."

"Then I learned something else about the man who took Elaine." I glanced at the firefighters, police officers, and EMTs admirably doing their jobs and swallowed at the knot of fear in my throat. "He wore coveralls that looked just like these. I think he's one of you."

## CHAPTER
# NINETEEN

There was an excellent chance that Elaine and possibly Penny were being held at Clark Faber's house. The home, it turned out, was on a five-acre plot less than four miles from where Elaine's car had been run off the road. Coincidence? I didn't think so. Of course, why had Elaine driven out this way? She was supposed to be going to her in-laws, not going out for a country drive.

Whatever the reason, we had a solid plan for getting the women back.

"I'll get the key from the station," Rob said. "Ezra and Nora, you guys drive up west of Faber's property and hide out of the way. When I get the call on where to drop the key, I'll text you. You all wait to see if the guy leaves. If he does, that's when you go in and get Elaine. And Penny, of course, if she's there too."

"What about his partner?" I asked. "He might be staying back to watch over the house."

Rob took off his ball cap and scratched his head. He reached down to his ankle and pulled up his pant leg. He unclipped a small gun from a strap, holster and all. "Here." He held it out to Ezra. "Use my Ruger." The weapon was smaller than Ezra's hand.

"I have my own weapon in the car." Ezra handed it to me. "Nora knows her way around a gun, and she has a concealed carry license. She can use your pea-shooter."

The pea-shooter in question was a Ruger LCP II and was light and comfortable in my hand. "Nice."

"Watch the rise on it," Rob said. "It can catch the meat at the base of your thumb if you're not careful. Also, it has an easy trigger, and there's no external safety, so keep it in the hard holster unless you need it."

"Now, I wish I would've brought my nine-millimeter from home. Had I known this was going to be that kind of vacation...." I let the implication lie as I put the gun inside my jacket. "I hope I don't need it." I was a crack shot when it came to targets, and I wasn't afraid to pull a weapon on someone threatening the people I love or me.

However, actually shooting a person, or any living creature for that matter, lacked a lot of appeal. "Thank you, Rob. I'll take good care of it."

Rob gave me an assessing look. "I have a feeling I'm underestimating you, Nora."

I gave him a sly smile. "You wouldn't be the first."

"Isn't that the truth," Ezra said. "So, we have a plan."

Rob nodded. "Yep, we have a plan." He glanced between us. "Keep your cell phones on and in silent mode. Vibration only."

Ezra arched a brow at his brother-in-law. "This isn't my first rodeo."

Rob raised a finger. "Just a minute." He tugged the back seat of his truck forward and took out a black bulletproof vest. "For Nora."

Ezra, for the first time, looked impressed. "Great idea," he said. "Let's get moving before this guy calls you."

His brother-in-law nodded. "Onward and upward."

"Good luck," I told Rob. "We'll text you the minute we get Elaine. And if you have that bastard in your sites, take his butt down."

Rob bared his teeth. With the beard, it made him look more feral wolf than human. "You guys give me the go-ahead, and I'm going to make him wish he'd never heard Elaine's name."

---

HALF AN HOUR LATER, Rob texted. He'd been instructed to bring the key to Lakeland Cove, a Corp of Engineer park north of town. He was told to put the key inside the watershed and leave. If all went well, the bad guy would message him where he could find Elaine once the exchange was made.

We had different plans. We had the real key, and we

were going to take it with us to the house. Rob was going to drop a fake key that looked similar, then hide until the bad guy arrived, and hopefully, by then, Ezra and I would have rescued his sister and cousin.

It was solid in its conception, but I also knew that the best-laid plans often went to hell in a handbasket. I prayed this wasn't one of those times.

We had parked about four hundred yards west of Faber's driveway in a flat space off the road that was behind a few trees. My SUV was a dark green, so unless the guy leaving looked hard, he wouldn't see us. Faber's home was a large two-story modern farmhouse with a paved driveway and a security gate. Fancy.

Ezra was drumming his thumbs against the steering wheel, anxious to get going. Patience was usually his strong suit, but not today. His mother had texted twice, and he'd ignored the first one, then texted back that when he *knew, she'd know* and to *please stop messaging.*

It was terse, but he wasn't wrong. He needed all of his focus on the task at hand. Finally, after a good five minutes, a full-sized black SUV turned left, going east toward town.

"This is it," Ezra said. "You ready?"

"Let's go." We could see the house through the woods, and we'd already decided we'd go through the tundra to get there instead of pulling into the driveway in case the partner was around. The bulletproof vest added a layer of warmth that I hadn't expected. For all my years around police officers, this was the only time

I'd ever worn one. It was a little bulky and heavier than a life vest, but it didn't drag me down.

Ezra motioned for me to stay behind him as we quickly made our way to the porch. The front door was locked. A good sign, by my estimation. It meant that the man who'd left had locked it behind him, so he'd probably been without his other half.

Yay, for our side.

Trouble was the modern house had modern locks. "How are we going to get inside?" I asked quietly.

Ezra motioned toward the right side of the house. "You go around that way, and I'll go this way, and we'll see if we can find an opening to get in. Text me if you find a way, and I'll come to you. Don't go inside without me."

"I won't," I promised. "You do the same. Don't go in without me."

He gave me a quick wink of assurance. "I wouldn't dream of it."

The siding was white, and I felt like a sore thumb against it in broad daylight. Faber had a stone patio that wound its way around to the back, but I stayed close to the house, checking every window to see if it was unlatched. There was a glass door toward the back that gave me a view of the kitchen. The lights were on, and I couldn't see anyone in there. The door was unlocked. I carefully let it close and eased my hand off the handle. Success. We had our way in.

I took my phone out of my pocket and started to

text Ezra, but a reflection in the glass door startled me. I jumped back, thinking it was someone inside and was kept upright by a man behind me. Someone I knew. "Howdy?" I whispered as I moved out of his grasp. He didn't try to stop me. "What are you doing here?"

Howdy kept his voice low, too. "Rob called. He asked if Rollo and I would give you guys some backup. In for a penny, in for a pound," he said. "Rollo went around the other side. He's probably found Ezra already."

"I hope we won't need the backup," I told him. "This door's open. Let me text Ezra."

"You go ahead," he said, "I'll meet you inside."

"Wait," I hissed. He didn't listen. "Crap." I typed my message to Ezra about the open door, but when I hit send, I got a red triangle that said, "message failed." Son of a gun! There were places at Ezra's where the cell-phone reception stunk, and this place, apparently, had the same problem.

Howdy came back and opened the door. "I found Elaine," he said. "She's in the study, handcuffed, and I can't get her loose." He waved me in. "Come on."

"I'll wait for Ezra," I told him. "I promised I wouldn't go in without him."

"Suit yourself." He shrugged. "I'm going to search the house and see if I can find Penny. Rollo's beside himself with worry." He raised his hands. "You know where Elaine is, so go ahead and wait for Ezra."

I tried my phone again. The signal was completely

gone. Stupid rural living! It was one of the only things I missed about the city.

What was taking Ezra so long? Maybe he'd found a way in and was trying to text me? Or maybe he'd gone in without me. He wouldn't, though, right?

My frustration level was at an all-time high. Dang, it. I walked around the back of the house. No Ezra. Next, I walked to the other side of the front. Still no Ezra. I checked the front door. It was open now. Had he and Rollo gone in?

I clenched my teeth, my jaw flexing. Thanks to the bulletproof vest, my body was warm, but my legs were getting colder, and even my feet were starting to ache with the beginnings of hypothermia. I uttered a few choice words at the universe and went inside. The heated house felt good on my bones. I nervously poked my head around corners, checking rooms, one by one, until I found the study with Elaine. Howdy had been right. She'd been handcuffed and gagged. Her eyes widened when she saw me.

I put my finger to my lips. "I'll be right back," I said. I'd picked a few handcuffs in my day. Perks of being married to and dating a cop. I just needed the right tools.

I hustled across the living room to the kitchen and started pulling out drawers. I needed a couple of paper clips or some stiff wire. I used to be good with a bobby pin, but I stopped wearing them years ago.

Howdy came into the kitchen.

"Did you find Penny?" I asked.

"I did," he said, "but I can't get to her." His brow pinched. "She's in a locked room that I can't get into."

I found the junk drawer and rummaged through it. "Have you seen Ezra and Rollo?"

"I think I heard them upstairs," he said. He came over to the drawer. "What are you looking for? Maybe I can help."

"I need something to pick those handcuffs."

He looked surprised. "You know how to pick handcuffs?" He leaned over and put his elbows on the counter. The position moved his jacket sleeve up, exposing his forearm.

"I do," I said calmly as I noticed a large jagged scar, very similar to the wound that I'd seen in my vision at Penny's apartment. Had that been Howdy's blood on the couch? Crap." Uh, what floor is Penny on?" I asked, trying to act nonchalant.

"The second one," he said. "But like I told you, I can't get to her."

Unable to find what I needed, I closed the drawer. "I'm going to go stay with Elaine until Ezra comes down." I had to get out of the kitchen and put some distance between us. Howdy was taller than me, and if he was Penny's mystery psychopath, I didn't want to be within arms reach of him.

"I'll go with you," he said.

Shoving my hand in my pocket to get the Ruger, I

picked up the pace. "No need," I said. "Ezra and Rollo can help you with Penny. You should go find them."

I was about ten feet from the study. If I hadn't been suspicious of Howdy at this point, the look of sheer terror on Elaine's face would've convinced me.

"Nora, wait," he said. "I've got something for you."

Fool me, I looked back over my shoulder. Howdy had a gun in his hand. "Courtesy of your boyfriend," he said jovially.

I ran then, sore knees be damned, and felt the bullet hit between my spine and shoulder blade. It spun me hard, and I landed face down inside the study.

"Two down," Howdy said. "One to go."

I held my breath as the horror of what his words implied soaked in. Had he already got to Ezra? I had to be still. The pain of getting shot was tremendous, even with a bulletproof vest on, but playing dead was the only way I was going to stay alive.

Elaine was screaming beneath her gag. Howdy laughed. "Don't worry, darling. I'll be back for you later."

CHAPTER

# TWENTY

I heard him walk away, happily whistling, "It's Beginning to Look a Lot Like Christmas," the creep. I stayed still for another minute to make sure he wasn't nearby. When I finally did move, it was sheer agony. Breathing had also taken on another level of excruciating. The impact had probably cracked my ribs.

Elaine's whimpers quieted when she saw me moving.

I put my finger to my lips. "Shhhh." I managed to get up to my knees, but holy crap, I was going to be sore for a month.

The door had a lock, so I closed it and turned the latch. As fast as I could, which was terribly slow, I limped over to Elaine and took her gag down. Her face was bruised and cut from where the airbag had exploded in her face. At least, I hope it had been all airbag. The way Faber had been beaten, this guy had a real sadistic streak. They'd handcuffed her behind her back, making it harder for her to move or escape.

"Did the lotion work?" she asked.

"Yes," I told her. "It worked like a charm. That was such smart thinking, especially after a terrible wreck."

She started crying. "My wrist is broken. My hand is swelling, and it's starting to go numb."

Before I helped her, I took the gun out of my jacket and took it out of its holster. Elaine's eyes shifted from my face to the Ruger.

"Courtesy of your husband," I told her.

"Is Rob here?"

I shook my head. "He's tracking down Howdy's partner. He'll be here soon." I hoped I wasn't wrong.

"Where's Easy?" she asked.

"He's coming too." That answer had been for me. I couldn't let myself believe anything else. Ezra was alive, and I knew no matter where he was, he was fighting to get to me.

"They want the key that you all found in the alley," Elaine said. "It opens a safe inside the panic room. I think Penny locked herself inside, and they haven't been able to get her out."

Howdy had said that he and Rollo had come as backup. Did that mean Rollo was involved? I hadn't gotten a creepy vibe from Rollo, but I hadn't with Howdy, either. The man was very good at masking his darkness.

Still, I had to know. "Do you know who Howdy's partner is?" I asked. "Is it Rollo?"

"No," Elaine said. "It's Tom-tom."

"I met him at the parade yesterday," I said. "A shorter man with a pig nose."

"That's him," Elaine confirmed. "His real name is Tommy Martin, and I've known him since we were little. Heck, I'm friends with his wife. I even went to their wedding. He'd texted me and told me that Rollo had broken down outside of town and needed a ride. I didn't even question it. Then the jerk ran me off the road. I had no idea it was him until he brought me here and took off his mask. I didn't know Howdy was involved until just a few minutes before you arrived." She shivered. "He said he was going to take his time doing terrible things to me, Nora. I'm so scared."

"I'm not going to let him touch you," I swore to her. "I'll blow his head off before he gets through the door." I examined her hand. It was turning purple, and it was hard to feel a pulse under all the swelling. "We have to get these cuffs off you."

"How?" Elaine asked. "Tom-tom took the keys with him when he left."

I got up and searched the room. There was a writing desk by a large window. There were Star Wars toys, books, and a special edition DVD set of the movies. Clark Faber had been the Chewbacca to Penny's Leia. I opened the front drawer on the desk and rejoiced at the sight of paperclips. "Yes!"

A picture caught my eye. I recognized Penny, but not the man with her. They were standing in front of a building that had Pike Manufacturing in big letters across a nearby sign. I took the picture and tucked it into my jacket, retrieved a paper clip, and went back to Elaine. "I'll have you out of this in no time."

"I don't want to sound ungrateful," she said, "but please hurry."

"You got it." I tucked my hair behind my ears and out of my face, then opened the paper clip and stuck the end into the keyhole. When it was in straight, I bent it forward, so the wire on the end would mimic the key. After a couple of misses, I finally caught the latch that lowered the teeth in the cuff bracelet, and it slid open.

Elaine let out a soft cry of relief. I made quick work of the other side and had her free in seconds.

"You're really good at that," she said.

"I'm a bit rusty," I told her. My dad had taught me with his cuffs, and I'd kept up the skill. I used to do the handcuff trick almost every weekend when Shawn and I were in college. You can win a lot of money at the bar, betting someone you could get out of handcuffs before they could chug a beer. I never lost.

"What now?" Elaine asked.

"Now." I dug my car keys from my jacket, and I handed her my phone. "My car is just up the road. If you exit the house and run to the right. About a hundred feet through the woods, you'll find it parked between two

197

trees. Use my phone and call the police, then get the hell out of here."

"What are you going to do?" she asked.

"I'm going to find Ezra, and we'll be right behind you." What I didn't tell her was that if I found Ezra dead, I was going to find Howdy and kill him.

I made certain the coast was clear, then I walked Elaine to the door and watched her from the window as she bolted for the woods. Good girl. Now it was time to find my partner.

---

FROM THE STAIRWELL, I heard Howdy sing, "Little Pen, little Pen, let me in." Then in a higher voice, he sang, "Not by the balls of my many, men, men."

There was no response to his taunts.

In a sweet, sincere tone, he pleaded, "Come on, Pen. I won't hurt you, I promise. Just open the door."

Again, there was no response.

The banging and the screaming that came next froze me in place. "Open the door, Penelope. Open the door! I don't want to hurt you, but I will!"

It's no wonder I never recognized his voice in the visions. It was like his voice had as many split personalities as he did. Penny seemed safe enough for now where she was, and she wasn't my primary concern. Ezra was the only person I wanted to find right now. The right side of my back blossomed with pain every time I turned or twisted. Between getting shot and the impact of my body hitting the floor, I was one big aching bruise. On top of that, the cracked ribs made my right arm weak. I was grateful the Ruger was small and light. Even so, I had to support it with my left hand if I wanted to lift it up.

I kept my finger next to the trigger but not on it. If Ezra did pop up, I didn't want to accidentally shoot him. God, I missed Gilly. I didn't know why my BFF popped into my head. Maybe because I hadn't been a good friend to her the last time we'd spoken. I truly was happy for her, and I had a good life with or without her living next door. Why had I had such selfish thoughts?

But what if Ezra was really gone? The saliva in my mouth was thick as fear tightened my throat. I couldn't think like that. I had to hold onto hope. I went back down the stairs, afraid that the slightest creak in the floor would give me away. Howdy thought I was dead and Elaine incapacitated. His focus was on Penny, and there was no better time to search the rooms on the main floor. A scratching noise, like mice in the wall, startled me. It was coming from behind a door at the end of a long hall.

Weapon ready, I slowly turned the knob, prepared to run away like a coward if it turned out to be actual mice. The sight at the bottom of the steps took my breath away.

"Ezra," I croaked. Adrenaline made my knees feel brand new as I ran down the staircase. His eyes were open, but he looked dazed. "Are you okay? Are you hurt? Can you stand?"

"Nora." He said my name on an exhale. "I thought I told you not to come inside without me."

"When we get out of this, I'm going to throat punch you," I scolded him.

"Looking forward to it." He got to an elbow. "Help me up."

"What happened?" I asked.

"Howdy surprised me," Ezra grunted as he got to his feet. "He hit me over the head, and the next thing I knew, I was at the bottom of these steps. I was struggling to pull myself up, then you appeared."

He had his arm around my shoulder, and I bit my tongue to keep him from knowing just how much pain I was in. My only priority was getting him out of this house and away from the sociopath.

"I found Elaine," I told him, gripping the pistol tightly so I wouldn't drop it.

"Is she okay?"

"Yes." We made it up a few steps. "I got her out of the house. If all has gone to plan, the cops are on their way, and she's halfway home by now."

Ezra's shoulders sagged. "Thank you."

"Howdy's accomplice is that guy Tom-tom from the parade."

"What do they want?"

"Money, love, torture, death, kill, all the usual. Penny has locked herself in a panic room upstairs, and Howdy's been trying to get her to come out. I think that's why he wants the key."

"How in the world did you learn all this?"

"I listened," I said. "Your sister told me some of it, and Howdy is upstairs ranting like a maniac trying to get Penny to come out and play."

We had finally made it to the top of the stairs. Ezra took his weight off me for a moment, so I could get the door, and I sagged with relief.

"Nora." His voice was full of alarm. "Why is there a bullet hole in the back of your coat?"

"Because I got shot," I told him. "We owe Rob a case of beer for the bulletproof vest. Now, there's a madman with your gun running around this place, so unless you want me to get shot again, let's save this conversation for later and get the heck out of here."

We'd made it a few steps down the hall when I heard from behind us, "And just like Lazarus, they arose from the dead." There was a metallic tap. "Now, turn around slowly. Both of you. I want to see just how righteous you are."

I didn't turn around. Instead, I said, "Practicing for your insanity defense, huh?"

Ezra's eyes widened at me. I held my hand in front of my body and moved my eyes from him to the Ruger.

"I don't mind shooting you in the back," Howdy said. "I think I've already proven that."

"Fine," I said. "We'll turn around, but first tell me,

why go through all this trouble? You got the money. Why didn't you run?"

"Because I want more money," he said.

"I think you're a liar," I told him.

He laughed. "And what was your first clue? Now turn around. I won't ask again. I'll just put a couple of bullets in your heads. And that's not a lie."

"Okay," Ezra said. "Just give me a minute. I'm a little banged up from being thrown down a flight of steps." He moved his hand to mine and took the gun. I pressed my hip against his body to prevent Howdy from seeing the exchange.

"Me first," I said. Slowly, I raised my hands and pivoted to face the man.

As Ezra began to turn, I let out a yelp and grabbed my side. Howdy swung the gun at me.

"I think my ribs poking into my lung," I said as I dramatically fell against the wall.

While Howdy's focus was on me, Ezra whipped around and fired. The bullet went wide and buried itself in the drywall.

"Son of a—" Howdy brought his gun up, but not before Ezra got another shot off. This one nailed the psychopath in the thigh. He howled with rage.

It was all fun and games until you were the one getting shot, I thought.

"Run, Nora," Ezra shouted.

I ran up the hall and into the kitchen. I grabbed a meat cleaver from a knife block, then went through the kitchen, into the living room, and around the corner to the opposite side of the hall. Two more shots rang out, and I didn't hesitate. I raced up the hall, cleaver held high. Ezra was on the ground, and Howdy was standing with his back to me. I wouldn't let him get off another shot.

I screamed with sheer madness as I lunged in his direction. Howdy turned to face me, his face shocked and ashen. A hole in his chest oozed blood down his shirt, and then he fell.

I blinked, waiting for Howdy, like a true horror villain, to pop back up for one last hurrah. It didn't happen.

I dropped the cleaver and ran to Ezra. "Are you shot? Did he shoot you?"

"Barely a graze," he said. "I won't even need stitches."

I smacked his shoulder, and we both said, "Ow."

I kissed him. "You scared the crap out of me. Never again, do you hear me? You are not allowed to die."

"I'll do my best to live forever," he smirked.

"See that you do." I kissed him again. Sirens blared, and the weight of fear lifted from my shoulders.

Rob was the first cop through the door. "Ezra! Nora!"

"We're here," Ezra yelled. I helped him to his feet.

Rob found us. He looked from us to the body on the floor. He bent down and checked Howdy for a pulse. "Damn," he said. "You two are not to be taken lightly.

There's an ambulance out front. Go get checked out. You look like hell."

I nodded. "Then it matches how I feel."

Ezra handed him the Ruger. "Thanks for the loan." He pointed to the downed criminal. "I'll expect mine back when you put this case to bed."

"You got it," Rob agreed. "I arrested Tommy Martin at the park."

"Good. I hope he rots in jail." I pointed to the stairs. "Penny's on the second floor," I told him. "The key fits some kind of safe up there. She's locked herself in a panic room to keep Howdy away from her. You should tell her she can come out now."

Rob snapped his fingers at the young, uniformed officer behind him. "Rogers," he said, "Get upstairs and check it out."

"Come on," Ezra said to me. "Let's get out of here."

"Wait a minute." I pulled the picture of Penny with the man from my jacket pocket. "Do you know who this is?"

"It's Penny," Rob said.

"Not her, the guy."

He frowned. "That's Carl Faber."

I shook my head. "That's not Carl Faber."

"What do you mean?"

Now that I'd gotten confirmation, one of the visions made a lot more sense to me. "We saw an old DMV photo of the real Carl Faber at the hospital today. This guy isn't him."

"You think he stole Carl Faber's identity?" Rob asked.

"I do." I thought about Carl's mother. "I think the real Carl Faber is dead. Maybe natural causes, and I think this guy took advantage of a woman with Alzheimer's to insert himself into a life that wasn't his and inherit a lot of money in the process." I looked down the hall where Officer Rogers was escorting Penny down the steps. I nodded in her direction. "Ask her who Kevin is," I said. "And I'll bet you dollars to donuts, her missing clothes are here."

"What about the stolen charity money?"

I inclined my head again toward Penny. "I think she had something to do with that as well, and then she fell for a funny little man who wanted to make a new life with her."

Rob sighed. "I'm going to have to arrest my wife's cousin, aren't I?"

"Probably," I said. "But I have a feeling she'll land on her feet."

"Like a cat with nine lives," Rob mused.

"More like a vampire." Ezra shook his head. "How in the world am I going to explain all this to Aunt Lettie?"

"You're not," I told him as I gave Rob a pat on the chest when we passed by. "That's a job for the police, and you don't have jurisdiction."

# TWENTY-ONE

The Holden family ended up spending the rest of Christmas eve at the hospital.

It turned out that Elaine had broken her wrist, and she'd ended up with a festive red and green cast for the holiday. I'd fractured two ribs and got a few pain pills for my efforts, and Ezra, under protest, needed four stitches where a bullet had grazed his shoulder. As bad as we all felt, tomorrow was going to be the real test of endurance.

Hal, Lynn, and Rob were in the emergency department's waiting area when the doctors finally released us.

When Rob's gaze met Elaine's, she practically ran into his arms. It was like something out of a Hallmark movie.

"I was so scared," he choked out. "I thought I would lose you."

"You'll never lose me." She kissed him many times. "I'm never letting you go again." And while it might be the pharmaceutical-grade narcotics the hospital had me on, I thought it was fantastically romantic. Elaine and Rob were getting a second chance love story, and it was wonderful.

Lynn gave me a, thankfully, brief and gentle hug. Even with the medications, I was still sore when touched. "Elaine told us how you saved her life." She took my hand and clasped it between hers. "I don't know if I'll ever be able to thank you enough."

"Elaine did all the hard work." I waved off the thanks. "I just picked the lock."

Ezra shook his head. "Nora is being modest. I'm not sure any of us would've gotten out without her quick thinking." He and his mother stared at each other for a moment. "Mom," he said.

"Son," she replied.

He put his arms around her and hugged her hard. "I forgive you, and I'm sorry, too. I hope you'll forgive me. I've spent too many years being mad at you. I don't want to do that anymore. I want us to be close again. To be a family."

Lynn's eyes shone with unshed tears. "I want that more than I can say." She held him tightly. "It's the best Christmas present I could ask for." She let him go and shook her head. "And after today, I think it's going to be all the Christmas any of us get. I didn't have any time to do dinner preparations today."

It could've been the drugs, but I had a lightbulb moment, and I wondered if I had one more Christmas rabbit I could pull out of a stocking hat.

"Maybe we can work some holiday magic." I glanced at Ezra and smiled. "How about a Holly Molly Christmas, eh?"

---

*December 25th, Christmas Day, and we all survived...*

MOLLY HIGGINS, the owner of the Thorny Creek Inn, had been eager to help when I told her about Ezra's family weekend. She said, and I quote, "The more, the merrier."

We called Lynn as soon as we had the thumbs up, and she started the phone tree to invite the rest of the family. The main house had a ballroom, and that's where Molly had put the Holdens for their family dinner.

Lynn, Hal, Lettie, Orsen, Rollo, and Baxter, along with their wives, Carla and Wendy, had arrived around noon. Lorena, Rose Marie and her son Ryan showed up. Rose Marie brought a date. It turned out she'd been dating Rollo's friend Blake. He was a little younger than her, and she'd worried her mother would ruin their relationship. She told me that Ezra and I had inspired her to finally come clean to Lorena.

Elaine and Rob, of course, along with Prissy and

Tessa, made it shortly after. Elaine's face was a little swollen and bruised, but considering what she'd been through, it could've turned out worse.

Penny wasn't there because she was still in the city jail. But from what Rob said, she would probably be out on Tuesday with bail. She would probably face some jail time for her part in the crimes, but whatever the outcome of her arrest, Lettie and Orsen were just happy she was safe.

Tom-tom, on the other hand, was looking at some serious time for assault with a deadly weapon, kidnapping, conspiracy, larceny, and a few other charges that I was certain a creative prosecuting attorney could tack on.

As to Clark Faber, Penny had reluctantly confirmed that his real name was Kevin Duncan. He had been in the military with the real Clark Faber, who died of a heart attack. He'd taken the dead man's identity to run away from a massive gambling debt he'd accumulated. According to Penny, though, Kevin took taking care of Faber's mom seriously. He'd cared for the woman and had grieved when she'd died. That was something, I supposed. They had planned to use Clark's inheritance to start over somewhere else. When Penny had been taken, he'd gone to the farmer's field in order to exchange the charity money for her freedom. Howdy, of course, had other plans.

Howdy, whose legal name was Jason Birdsong, aka

Jaybird, had grown up in the same neighborhood as the real Faber, and that's when his plan to rob the imposter blind had formed. He'd employed his then-girlfriend, Penny, to get close to the man and learn his secrets. What Penny ended up learning was that she wanted to be with someone sweet like Kevin, even if he was an identity thief and not an abusive jerk like Howdy. I wasn't sad Howdy was dead. The world was a little less terrifying without him in it.

Christmas carols played softly in the background. I'd made sure everyone got lotions, soaps, and gift boxes from Scents and Scentsability. Ezra was laughing and joking with his cousins and his sister, and while I'd seen him happy plenty of times, I don't know that I'd ever seen him quite so joyous.

Lorena walked over to me, holding a cranberry mint gift set that included lotion, hand-crafted soaps, and a body spray. "This is pretty nice," she said to me. I waited for the follow-up zinger, but it didn't come.

"Thanks," I told her. "It's one of my shop's best-selling holiday scents."

"I'm not talking about the gift." She shook her head. "When Ezra left, he broke his mother's heart. She'd hoped when Mason graduated, he'd move back, and she'd have her son home again. But I can see how much he cares for you." Her gaze flicked to mine then she rolled her eyes. "How much he loves you. So, I just wanted to say I'm sorry for being a crabby ass."

"Are you...being nice?" I teased.

Lorena smirked. "What if I am?"

"I'd say it's a freaking Christmas miracle."

The woman let out a guffaw that would've startled the ghost of Christmas past. "I like you, Nora. You're not a simp."

"I like you too, Lorena. You're hilarious."

Ezra made his way to us. "Ari's ready," he said.

I rubbed my hands together. "Yay." Ari, our technical genius, had set up a video call for us with all our family in Garden Cove. Ezra set a tablet on the dining table.

I'll admit, I teared up when Gilly, Scott, Marco, and Ari appeared on the screen. "Merry Christmas, Aunt Nora," the twins said in unison.

I waved to them. Then Pippa, Jordy, and J.J. showed up in their own box as the screen split. "Happiest of Holidays, Ezra and Nora," Pippa said. "And the whole Holden family!"

The whole Holden family came around the back of us and wished their good tidings to my family. And finally, Mason popped into a box at the bottom center.

"Hey, Dad and Nora. Merry Christmas."

Ezra beamed. "Happy Christmas, kid," he said. "I can't wait to see you tomorrow."

"You too, Dad," Mason told him. "Hi, Grandma and Grandpa Holden," he added. "Merry Christmas."

Lynn and Hal waved, and Lynn blew kisses.

Gilly shook her head at me and said, "Can you go one holiday without getting in trouble?"

I snickered. "I certainly hope so." We all talked for a little while, then said our love and goodbyes.

Lynn looped elbows with her son. "You've made a wonderful life for yourself," she told him. "I can't wait to be a part of it."

He patted his mother's hand. "You guys are coming to Garden Cove for New Year's Eve, right?"

"Is this a whole family invitation?" Elaine asked. "Because you'll have to get a restraining order to keep me away."

They all laughed together, and I wished I could bottle the memory and take it out whenever I needed a cheer.

Ezra took my hand, and we strolled over to the mistletoe. "Any excuse to kiss you is a good one." He pressed his mouth to mine, and the warmth and tenderness of his lips made me feel as if I were floating. Of course, it could've been the drugs. I'd had to take a pill just to get out of bed that morning.

When the kiss ended, I pressed my palm to his cheek. "I love you."

"Not as much as I love you."

"We'll call it a tie."

He touched his forehead to mine. "Deal."

Our hostess Molly, along with her chef—who turned out to be her son—rolled a giant honey ham and a roasted turkey out into the room. "Dinner is served," she said with a brightness that lifted the room. "Take your seats, and we'll get you all set up."

My mouth watered as she brought out scalloped potatoes, green beans with candied bacon, stuffed butternut squash, cranberry gelatin, whipped cream salad, and Parker House rolls. It was a feast fit for a family.

"Merry Christmas, everyone," Molly said.

In near-perfect unison, the table rejoined, "Merry Christmas!"

*And to all, a Happy New Year.*

*Nora Black*

The end

**Read the next book!**

**Book 8 – The Vapes of Wrath**

**My name is Nora Black, and I'm celebrating my BFFs midlife matrimony!**

Gilly is engaged, and I have invited a couple of friends to help us celebrate her bachelorette vacation in wine country. We are leaving work behind for three days of good food, good friends, and good fun.

Or so I thought. When the youngest of our group, Tippi Davenport, gets flirty with a local musician, his girlfriend is less than pleased. Some might even call her reaction homicidal. But when the woman turns up dead during a hiking tour, our vacation turns into an investigation.

It doesn't take a sommelier to sniff out the sour grapes surrounding this murder, including the astringent scents of old money, family intrigue, jealousy, and greed. I'll have to employ my psychic nose to catch a killer and get the bride back home to Garden Cove in time for her wedding.

# THE VAPES OF WRATH - CHAPTER 1

"Oh my gosh," Tippi Davenport exclaimed. "This place has a freaking spiral staircase up to the loft. Can I have that room?"

"Yes," Gilly, Pippa, and I all said simultaneously. I was as adventurous as the next fifty-four-year-old, but there was no way I would be climbing up and down twenty steps of a circular maze every morning and night for the next two and a half days.

There were three other bedrooms in River Bluff House on the Rivière Tranquille Vineyard's property. The vineyard had been established in 1934 by Vigneron Rigel Nichols, a British expatriate who'd stayed in France after World War I to learn the art of winemaking. He relocated to the small Midwest town of Marseille—Missouri; the local pronunciation was Mar-sail, not the French Maa-say—to start his own label. According to the website, the place was still family-owned and operated. I'd booked us a three-day midweek package to celebrate my best friend's upcoming wedding.

After kissing a lot of toads over the years, my BFF Gilly Martin had finally found herself a Dr. Charming. On Saturday, four days from now, she would officially become Gilly Graham. Scott Graham, an emergency room doctor, was the whole package—friendly, handsome, professional, and, most importantly, treated Gilly like a real partner.

I couldn't be happier for her. At least, that was the act I was putting on. Don't get me wrong, I was thrilled for Gilly, and I knew Scott would spend the rest of his life making her happy. Still, I would miss having her next door. I'd moved over to Gilly's neighborhood so that we could spend more time together. But between work, spending most of my free time with my guy Ezra, and consulting on the occasional criminal case with the Garden Cove PD, I'll admit we hadn't seen as much of each other as I'd expected. Still, it had been nice knowing she was there.

I tucked my insecurities away as I gestured at the chunky, comfortable furniture, the hardwood floors, the upgraded kitchen, and the large balcony. I gave a sigh of relief. "The place looks just like its pictures." That wasn't always the case when you booked from a website.

Pippa's blonde ponytail bobbed as she nodded her agreement. "I can't believe I have two whole days without J.J., the dogs, and Jordy. Lord help me, I love them all to pieces, but sometimes a girl needs a few days of no responsibility." Her hips were fuller since having her daughter, but Pippa's delicate bone structure and willowy height made her look rail thin.

"Amen!" Tippi, who was the mini-me for Pippa—same fine bones, same height, and same blonde hair—exclaimed from the loft. "We are wild and carefree."

"Not too wild or carefree," Pippa cautioned her younger sister.

Since moving to Garden Cove two years earlier, Tippi had worked almost full-time as her sister Pippa's nanny. The move and the job had changed the younger woman's life in many ways. For one, she'd gotten and stayed sober.

The irony that we were at a vineyard, and Tippi was our sober buddy, was not lost on me. She'd insisted she could handle it. I hoped for her sake and Pippa's that she was right.

Tippi came back down to the living room. She grabbed her large suitcase and hauled it up the spiral stairs, making me so happy I hadn't been saddled with that space. Tippi was in her mid-thirties and life-cycled daily for exercise. She could handle the impact on her joints better than those of us in the over-40 crowd. Not that I wasn't active. I walked three miles every morning, barring bad weather. Between that and the shots in my knees, I didn't have much trouble. Still, it was better not to add to the wear and tear if I could help it. As my mother used to point out, you only get one body, so it pays to take care of it.

We scoped out the other bedrooms. I was pleased by the scent of crisp pine cleaner and bleach. It meant my smell-o-vision, aka my psychic nose, was less likely to be active. Unless someone had a strong emotional connection to the aroma of cleaning products, I was safe from other people's memories for the moment.

Pippa and I took the two queen suites, and Gilly, as the bride-to-be, took the main king suite. All the bedrooms, including the loft, had private bathrooms, but only Gilly's included a large free-standing tub. It was fine by me. I preferred a shower, anyhow.

"You can see the river from the bathroom," Gilly called out. "The view is spectacular." She slung her arms around me from behind. "It's perfect!" She gave me a conspiratorial look. "Where are you hiding the strippers?"

"I told you. No strippers. It's not that kind of a bachelorette."

"Fine," she huffed. "But I would've ordered you a few strippers." She laughed all the way to her room.

I smiled as I went into my room, unpacked my suitcase, and put my toiletries in my en suite. It was after five, and as the maid of honor, I'd planned this getaway to a T. "We have reservations for dinner at La Sous Terre in an hour. Dress is classy casual."

Pippa popped her head into my room. "Can I just say again how excited I am for a grown-up getaway?"

I grinned. "You can say it as many times as you like."

Forty minutes later, we were at La Sous Terre. The exterior was a combination of stone and stucco, with a large sweeping roof that gave it a French country vibe. We were dressed to the sevens for the evening and with time to spare before our reservation. Unfortunately, that meant we had to wait at the bar for our table to open. Fortunately, the place had live music from a band called the Ray-tones, and they weren't half bad for a local four-piece cover band.

The lead guitarist, who also doubled as the lead vocalist, crooned Bob Seger's "Night Moves" to five enrapt tables of swaying fans near the small stage area.

Tippi sat on the barstool to my right. She leaned over until our shoulders were touching and muttered, "Hot damn, he's cute."

She wasn't wrong. He was clean-shaven and looked to be in his mid-thirties, but with the chiseled jawline of a high school quarterback. He wore a tight black t-shirt that showed off his muscled arms and chest and even tighter jeans that showed off his other assets.

Two of the five tables were crowded with women wearing black t-shirts with Ray-tones written in fancy lettering on the backs. They were chair dancing as they sang along to his every word. "Looks like he has a fan club. I'm sure they'll let you join." One of the tables had a stack of CDs and t-shirts for sale. "They even have merch if you want to follow him on the road."

Gilly snorted a laugh, and Tippi gave me a sour look. "I just said he was cute."

I fought the grin tugging at my lips. "And you aren't wrong," I conceded. "He's cute."

The bartender, the woman who had checked us in for our house when we arrived, finally came over and took our drink order. Two white wines, one red, and one sparkling grape juice.

"Black, party of four?" a young woman in blue with a white apron asked.

"That's us," I told her.

She held a stack of menus under her arm. "Your table is ready."

"What about the drinks?" Gilly asked.

"I'll stay for them," Tippi offered. "It shouldn't take too long. It's not like we ordered anything complicated. You guys get settled at the table."

"Sounds good." I gave her a grateful smile.

I'd requested a table with a view and was happy when they put us in front of a large window with a view of the vineyard and away from the music. We could still hear it, but it wasn't nearly as loud as at the bar. The delicious scent of sauteed vegetables and roasted meats made my mouth water. Luckily, I'd only had to suppress a few scent-related visions. I'd been working on visualizing walls whenever an unwanted, private memory popped into my head. It helped to some extent, but I still caught the occasional glimpses, and sometimes the emotion behind the memories was too strong to shove away.

"Good evening," the waitress greeted us as we sat down. "I'm Donna, and I'll be your server tonight. Can I start you off with some drinks?"

"We have some wine coming," Gilly said, "but we'd like ice water for everyone as well."

"You got it," Donna remarked. "Ice waters coming up. I'll be back to take your order then."

"Sounds good," I told her. The menus were fancy one-page inserts in leather holders with a four-course selection menu. The appetizers section listed goat cheese and almond-stuffed dates drizzled with burgundy syrup, crab-stuffed grape leaves with champagne butter sauce, and grilled garlic shrimp in a white wine reduction.

"These appetizers sound to die for," Gilly said. "I'm jazzed to try the stuffed dates. It sounds like the perfect blend of savory, tangy, and sweet."

I wasn't a fan of goat cheese. "I think I'll go for the crab-stuffed grape leaves."

Gilly's lower lip jutted slightly. "I wish Ari could've made it."

"She's solidifying her future," I reminded her. Gilly's daughter Ari had been working a summer internship with a colossal cybersecurity firm in Chicago. The girl was whip-smart, a virtual tech savant. "And she's driving home on Friday, so she'll be here for the wedding."

"I know." Gilly sighed. "I just miss her."

I patted Gilly's hand and then glanced over at Pippa. My blonde bestie's brow was knitted in a worried frown. "What's wrong?" I asked her. "Are you missing J.J. and Jordy?"

She shook her head and glanced at the bar where Tippi waited for the drinks. "All this food has alcohol in it," she said.

Gilly put her hand on Pippa's arm. "The alcohol is burned out of the sauces during cooking, but I'm sure they'll leave them off if Tippi is worried."

Pippa raised her brow. "I'm worried Tippi isn't worried enough."

"Do you think she's drinking again?" I asked.

Pippa was a good thirteen years younger than me, but the way she made everyone and everything her responsibility made her seem older. She'd started as my employee and had become one of my best friends. She was the first one I called when I'd decided to open a beauty supply salon in Garden Cove. Three years later, she was my business partner, and our little shop, with online sales and a big client who bought our lotions in bulk, was doing a lucrative business. Her sense of responsibility made her a business asset, but it could get in the way of her enjoying life.

"Tippi is going to make her own choices," I said. "We can hope she makes good ones, but you can't beat yourself up if she doesn't. Those decisions aren't about you."

Pippa sighed as she rubbed the tip of her index

finger along the wood grain on the table. "I know." Her expression was bleak. "She lives in my home, and I trust her with the care of my daughter. For the past two years, she's been in a controlled environment. If she isn't going to a meeting in her free time, she's talking with her sponsor or Jordy. This will be the first time she'll have to face alcohol without a buffer. If she falls off the wagon, I don't know where that leaves us. I love her. I'll continue to love her. But I don't know if I can have her around if she starts drinking again."

I gave my friend a soft smile. "How about we give Tippi the benefit of the doubt until she gives us a reason not to trust her?"

"You're right." Pippa leaned back in her chair. "I'll try to relax."

"You better," Gilly told her. "This is my special getaway, and I don't want any drama."

I'd been so focused on Pippa's worries that I hadn't noticed the music stopped playing until a woman shouted, "I'll kill you!"

We all turned wide-eyed to the bar and saw Tippi getting berated by a short blonde, who was being held back by the band's guitar player.

I glanced at Gilly as the three of us exited our seats. "Drama always seems to find a way," I told her.

She gave me a thin-lipped grimace. "Every. Freaking. Time."

**Read Book 8 – The Vapes of Wrath today!**

# ABOUT THE AUTHOR

I am a USA Today Bestselling author who writes paranormal mysteries and romances because I love all things whodunit, Otherworldly, and weird. Also, I wish my pittie, the adorable Kona Princess Warrior and my two cats Ash and Simon could talk. Or at least be more like Scooby-Doo and help me unmask villains at the haunted house up the street.

When I'm not writing about mystery-solving were-cougars or the adventures of a hapless psychic living among shapeshifters, I am preyed upon by stray kittens who end up living in my house because I can't say no to those sweet, furry faces. (Someone stop telling them where I live!)

I live in Mid-Missouri with my family and I spend my non-writing time doing really cool stuff...like watching TV and cleaning up dog poop

**Follow Renee!**
Bookbub
Renee's Rebel Readers FB Group
Newsletter